MW01230068

Once U|

By Duncan Wilson

Copyright © 2019 by Duncan Wilson

Cover Art By
Jose Castañeda

Old Mrs. Habernathy went about her morning routine with the diligence of one who had long ago etched her motions into hallowed traditions and her traditions into venerable monuments of regularity. Her life for the last five decades had been in this house, and the house was only a few years older than her occupation of it, making it the younger of the pair. It had served her well, rarely causing her any vexation, likely as it did not dare to upset her. The house was locked in a mutual competition with Old Mrs. Habernathy as to who would outlast the other. Most of the residents of the lane were betting on Old Mrs. Habernathy.

Having completed her rituals before the dawn, as she always did, Old Mrs. Habernathy settled down on her porch swing with a large kettle of tea on the table next to her and got out her knitting. She would not move from that spot except for meals the rest of the day. As the clocks in her house, of which there were hundreds, all chimed fifteen minutes to eight, she looked up to see Paxton Green walking briskly up the lane toward her house at the end of the cul-de-sac. She nodded imperceptibly to no one in particular. He was right on time as always. Being the only resident of the lane who had been there longer than herself, she seemed to extend a begrudging respect for the elderly widower, even if he did keep the most garish flower garden in the city and was an impossible man to manage. He was one of the last great untamable lions of masculinity, by the reckoning of those that knew him. No one now on the lane had ever known Mrs. Green. Her passing had preceded Old Mrs. Habernathy's arrival into the world, much less to the lane, and everyone else on the lane had arrived after Old Mrs. Habernathy.

Paxton Green strode right past her house as he rounded the end of the lane on his morning walk, nodding politely toward her as he always did and ignoring her sardonic grunt of acknowledgement. As he headed down the opposite side of the lane, his confident powerful strides were automatic, as his attention was entirely devoted to the lawns of his neighbors. There was not a change that went unnoticed in the topiaries and flowerbeds of the entire lane, so rapt and detailed was his examination, all while conducting his morning walk. He was not being nosey or spying on his neighbors, that was what the lane had Old Mrs. Habernathy for. Rather, his interest was entirely of the master hobbyist. Lawns and gardens were not only his one abiding passion in life, they had been honed over the last seven decades into his personal art. He examined his neighbors' yards not to steal their ideas, no indeed.

When he got home, as he did every morning after his walk, he poured himself a strong cup of coffee and sat down to several hours of writing. In brief, but articulate and polite, language he noted any peculiarities or missteps of each yard on the lane, and then proceeded to detail various suggestions and tips for how to improve upon or entirely revolutionize the landscaping in question. Once this series of missives was scripted, he placed each in its own envelope with the name of the homeowner on the outside, then handed them to Young Tommy, who stopped by Mr. Green's house every morning at eleven for just this task. They would be distributed to the whole lane over the next hour. After this had been accomplished, Paxton Green ate a light lunch before setting out into his garden for the remainder of the day. It was in his garden that he could be found each and every day, lovingly coaxing it into the most wondrous forms ever seen by his neighbors, as he had been for the last seventy years.

Young Tommy, who was actually well into his forties, took these unstamped letters and added them to his postal bag with the other correspondence for the lane, having long ago resigned himself to this peculiar and unofficial task on behalf of the eminent Paxton Green. It had been Mr. Green who had saddled Young Tommy with his misleading sobriquet, albeit at a time it would have been far more properly applicable. Young Tommy had grown up on the lane, and had become its mailman shortly after achieving majority. It was only a subsection of his total route, but it was by far the portion he looked forward to the most, as these homes were of his family and neighbors. It was always warm smiles and handshakes, and even the occasional hug that greeted him as he delivered the dispatches from the world outside of the lane. There were only two houses he could ever expect to be greeted with less than congeniality. There was, naturally, Old Mrs. Habernathy, whom he was always respectful to yet from whom he never anticipated more than a disinterested grunt and a wary eye. Of course, since she rarely received letters, not even the spam that everyone always received, he did not often have the opportunity to endure her icy reception.

The other house where Young Tommy never got a cordial salutation was the only other house, other than Old Mrs. Habernathy's, that Paxton Green never wrote yard advice for. Several houses in from the end of the cul-de-sac, on the east side of the lane, sat a lonesome graying ruin of a structure, the house with the dead yard. The trees in the yard, a yard which could never even generously be called a lawn, stood dead, having been planted some time around the building of the house itself, and never maintained since that time. There were a series of creepers that appeared to have attempted to colonize the walls of the ancient residence, but they too had presumably withered and died at various points in their conquests. The whole lot stood in stark contrast with all of the homes around it, each adorned with a garden or lawn of some level of magnificence depending on how much of Mr. Green's guidance had been followed. Even the animals avoided the house with the dead yard.

Young Tommy never liked picking up letters from this address, not because of its creepy demeanor, he'd seen houses in as ill repair elsewhere, and they were often far more cozy than their dilapidated exteriors let on. It was not the air of unease and the lack of life of the landscaping, though it was unnerving to see such sharp lines of life and non-life side by side like this. It was that no one ever entered nor left. The house was not abandoned, far from it, there were always strange noises emanating from within at random times of the day, often unidentifiable sounds that frightened birds and small children. As well, when Young Tommy picked up the letters patiently awaiting him from the box on the wall next to the front door, he could always hear the creaking floorboards of the entryway as someone, or something, moved about within. The mailman could not be certain it was a human that made this noise, as he imagined he could occasionally hear panting and the clacking of claws on wood. No one even knew who owned the house with the dead yard, as all correspondence that came from it had only the required number and street as the return address. Neatly printed, but not by any machine, with an ink that seemed to glow if you looked at it just right. There was never a name with the address. A few discreet enquiries by concerned residents of the lane with the city authorities had resulted in even more unanswered questions.

After picking up the one solitary grey letter from the house with the dead yard this morning, Young Tommy hurriedly moved on to the next house down, which belonged to the lane's resident professor. Wilber Tumbleburry was not employed as a teacher at any university or institute of education, nor was he employed in any fashion by anyone, and had not been at any time in the past. Rather, he was an heir to a moderate but handsome fortune from more industrious ancestors, who spent the years of his life accumulating knowledge for knowledge's sake. He was a professor of no particular subject, and at the same time, a professor of all of them. It was theorized by some of his more erudite neighbors that Wilber Tumbleburry likely knew more about any particular discipline than any other outside of that discipline's experts, and knew about any of them just less than would be necessary to be useful to any of those disciplines. It was a marvel to some just how much time and effort one man had dedicated to the art of being equally adept and useless at everything. Still, he was popular at parties, as he was relied upon to settle most any argument and always had some particularly fascinating story or news about some obscure science or craft to liven up any social gathering.

Young Tommy walked up the professor's path to find the middle aged scholar standing on his porch in his bathrobe, coffee mug in hand, regarding the decrepit structure next to his. Turning and nodding to Young Tommy as he approached him, Wilber Tumbleburry raised his mug by way of greeting. Clearing his throat of the morning's phlegm, Wilber greeted the lane's mailman, "Good morning to you! Another mystery letter from the mystery house?"

Young Tommy nodded as he handed Wilber his mail, replying, "Yep. How'd you know it was only one?"

"You'll have to pardon me my peccadillo, Young Tommy, but I've been noting every time you pick up mail there."

"But they don't always send just one letter."

"Indeed not! However, there is a pattern. They send one letter, then they send three letters fifteen days later, then six letters two days after that, then one letter two days later, then another twenty days before they once again send one letter."

Young Tommy scratched his head as he tried to follow along or remember if this accounting was accurate, but quickly gave up and just whistled, "As regular as that?"

"Without fail."

"That's quite something, professor. If you take into account the occasional bad weather days when the post office halts our routes, I don't see how it could be that consistent."

"Neither do I, and yet it is. This is the truly amazing aspect of the matter." The professor nodded eagerly and his eyes went wistful as if he were suddenly drawn into the most scintillating of contemplations of the potentialities of this mystery. Young Tommy just frowned and waved goodbye as he made his way across the street, glancing back every so often at the strange house, troubled by this revelation of regularity of letters posted from the house with the dead yard. It made no sense to him, so he tried to put it out of his mind rather than dwell on it as he approached the porch of the house across the lane. This well-appointed residence, with well-appointed floriculture that made Mr. Green beam with pride every time he wrote a brief congratulatory note to the residents, belonged to Ella and Ida. Young Tommy liked Ella and Ida, as did most everyone who ever met Ella and Ida. This near universal fondness was entirely the blame of Ella and Ida's congeniality and conviviality, incontestably manifest in the most delicious baked goods that were readily proffered to any and all they came in contact with.

This morning, these delectable delicacies took the form of a tray of ginger snaps held out to the approaching Young Tommy by Ida, who was sitting on the porch swing, enjoying the early morning coolness and reading some dense gaelic tome Young Tommy could not even read the name of. Young Tommy grinned as he handed Ida her mail with one hand and took a cookie from the tray with the other. He salivated at the mere sight of the treats, as he knew they would be peerless. He cheerfully thanked her, "Morning Ida! Thank you so much!"

Ida waved off his thanks, as she always did, as if anyone could so easily and regularly bake such scrumptious confections, responding instead, "How is the lane today, Young Tommy?"

"Same as it always is, Ida! Idyllic."

"Same as it always is, yes."

The door lazily swung open and Ella stumbled out, yawning. Ella slumped down on the swing next to Ida and grumbled incoherently about mornings and what particular class of animals they were for. Young Tommy nodded to the still bleary Ella, who gave a little wave in reply as she stifled yet another yawn, and headed back down the path to continue his deliveries.

"Morning, Ella dear," Ida's voice had a hint of bemusement, as it always did during this ritual.

"Morning..."

"How was your sleep?"

"Brief, restless, and full of strange dreams that upon reflection meant nothing."

"I asked about your sleep, not your life."

Ella yawned for the dozenth time that morning as she simultaneously groaned. Every morning it was the same tired joke, every morning it was just as bemoaned as the last, yet they both still engaged in the tradition as it was as much a part of their mutual identity as their baked goods and their undying love for one another.

Ella blinked a few more times before her vision became useful, and she stretched as she asked Ida, "Any new or notable sounds this morning?"

Ida shook her head, "Nope, dead silence this morning."

"That's odd."

"It's happened before."

"Not often, as I recall."

"No, not often, but occasionally."

They both sat silently regarding the house with the dead yard across the road as the birds, in their own horticultural paradise, competed with the buzzing of the bees to serenade the cresting of the sun in the sky. They made a regular activity of observing the unnatural auditory emissions of the old house, proceduralizing as much as possible the peculiar abeyance the house had presented from time immemorial. Ella and Ida had moved onto the lane a few decades after Old Mrs. Habernathy, but they were still only the fourth longest remaining dwellers of the lane. As far as they had been able to piece together, the house with the dead yard held the oldest resident or residents of the lane, but no one could attest to having ever seen them. The perpetual mystery of the residence piqued their curiosity, as it did everyone's, but like all of the others, they were not nearly as intrusive as to take the matter beyond idle observation. Truth be told, many of the residents were a little afraid of the enigmatic abode. Most, but not Ida. Being closer than the rest to the foreboding structure had bred in her, like it had in the professor, more of a familiar fascination than any trepidation.

As they discussed the other customary matters of life, they smiled at the youngest Murphy boy who came running up to their porch for a cookie. They liked the youngest Murphy boy, even if they did not care for his father. Not many on the lane cared for Mr. Murphy, but no one had to. Mr. Murphy cared enough about himself to make up the difference. His youngest son, on the other hand, was a preternaturally friendly young boy who was adored by every adult on the lane. Despite, or occasionally because of, the boy's mischievousness, he was welcome in each and every home on the lane, except Old Mrs. Habernathy's, though she too seemed fond of the little scamp in her own gruff way.

The youngest Murphy boy grabbed three cookies, despite a reprimanding cluck from the couple on the porch, and ran off toward his best friend Bobby's house. He always took two extra of everything Ella and Ida made, but not for himself, as the couple always thought. The youngest Murphy boy dashed through the back kitchen door of Bobby's house, shouting a cheery hello at Bobby's mom as he passed by in a blur. Stomping up the stairs as fast and as loud as he could, he shouted down the hall to Bobby that he had arrived before letting himself into the twins' room. Grinning like a maniac, he chirped hello to the twins and their faces lit up in delight. The youngest Murphy boy was one of the highlights of their day. He never failed to bring them such delicious treats and then would spend the next hour rambling on about what he had done the day before. The youngest Murphy boy was a terrible story teller, and would usually hop about in his narrative without rhyme or reason as he recalled some specific detail he had forgotten to mention before, but the twins cherished everything he said. What they were incapable of communicating with words or other means of expression they beamed forth in ear-to-ear grins as they listened raptly to the boy relate the inconsequentialities of his daily adventures outside while he fed them the cookies.

After a while, as usual, Bobby's mother came into the room and shooed the youngest Murphy boy out so she could shift the twins into sleeping positions. Bobby was waiting outside and the pair scampered down the stairs and outside to go adventuring somewhere along the lane, often in some unsuspecting neighbor's back yard or shed. The only place they never played was near the house with the dead yard. As they energetically ran down the sidewalk, the boys almost ran into and over Leo Tuttle. Barely twisting in time to allow the passage of the pair, Leo Tuttle squawked.

A man of a particularly nervous disposition, Leo Tuttle was quite prone to accidents of the usual and unusual variety, and as such was overly cautious about all of his movements and actions, not that this did much to alleviate his peculiar personal affliction of mishaps. As the young boys darted past with almost no room to spare and no worries in the world, Leo started into an awkward dance designed to keep him on his feet as he staggered to and fro like a drunken sailor, reeling. It took a full minute for him to regain his balance, a miraculous outcome especially considering the box he held was large and unwieldy and seemed to have a mind of its own as to which direction it would be heading at any moment. Upon fully recovering his footing and having stilled the box's independent movement, Leo Tuttle sighed in relief and shushed the box when it growled menacingly.

Leo Tuttle continued down the lane toward his own home, eyeing the house with the dead yard warily as he passed, never having trusted any place without some form of life. He customarily nodded with a smile to Ida and Ella as well, having nothing but appreciation for the couple, since upon more than one occasion he had received aid from them when one of his more calamitous mishaps struck. As he approached his own house at the end of the lane, his wary gaze shifted from the house with the dead yard to his less-than-amenable neighbor on the left, Old Mrs. Habernathy. His relations with Old Mrs. Habernathy were guarded at best, which was as good as anyone could hope to have with the aged spinster. Leo Tuttle kept his lawn well tended, thanks to the never-ending tips and encouragement from Paxton Green, and his fence well mended. He had consistently given Old Mrs. Habernathy no adequate excuse to complain, but was still often the recipient of her disapproving looks.

As he kept an eye on his less-than-sociable neighbor keeping an eye on him, Leo Tuttle stepped onto his porch and set down his parcel. It made a low sound as if it meant to growl again, but then fell silent. As he unlocked and opened his door, Leo Tuttle was startled by a hail from his neighbor from the other side. He turned and smiled at Jane, who had just exited the house with the pink vinyl siding and burnt umber trim and was jogging in place. Leo Tuttle liked Jane, a recent arrival on the lane. Young, vibrant, and full of energy, Jane was all smiles and waves to everyone on the lane, even Old Mrs. Habernathy, and her energy was infectious. Leo Tuttle waved to the young woman and greeted her, "Out for your 'morning' jog?"

"Yep!" Jane responded with a smile to the statement of the obvious, as she did with everyone. She turned and set out down the lane as Leo Tuttle picked up his large box and entered his house. Jane always jogged every morning, or mid-day on the weekends, having found that the air on the lane suited her exercise regimen far better than it had at her old place. Her pace was intense, and very quickly she had passed the house with the dead yard, had passed by Bobby's house, and was rapidly approaching Paxton Green's majestic yard, a highlight both coming and going on her morning jog. Mr. Green waved and bellowed a cheery hello to Jane as she ran past, a greeting she always returned with enthusiasm. The old man was set in his ways, but fortunately for everyone, those ways were congenial and warm.

Jane kept jogging, passing the youngest Murphy boy and Bobby as they were playing with something in the bushes, and even catching up to and passing Young Tommy, who tipped his hat to her as she flew by. Young Tommy was making good progress this morning, since most of the residents were still fast asleep as was customary on a weekend, which markedly decreased the amount of time he spent at each home. Young Tommy watched Jane as she went, marveling at the constant energy and enthusiasm she always seemed to have, then turned in to the house with the pink pelican statues. Before he reached the front door, a strained bellow of 'Come in!' escaped the home, and Young Tommy obligingly opened the unlocked door and entered

Liola's house. He paused to wipe his shoes on the rug and take off his hat, a convention he never forgot, and entered the 'room'. It had once been a sitting room, but over time had been converted into a library, a study, a bedroom, and a dining room all at the same time, as Liola's needs dictated. While he had never seen these changes taking place, Young Tommy occasionally noticed some new object or piece of furniture that had succumbed to the specific gravity of the 'room' and migrated there from elsewhere in the house.

Liola was where she always was when Young Tommy delivered her mail, in her chair. The chair had as much character as its resident, and Young Tommy had to wonder at its craftsmanship to have survived the many decades of almost constant occupation. Liola was grabbing a book off of a shelf behind her with her grabbing stick when Young Tommy greeted her. Hesitating in her present task, Liola turned her head and nodded acknowledgement, before going back to her struggle with the stick. Young Tommy waited for her to finish retrieving the tome, knowing better than to attempt to help, having well learned that lesson before. When she had the book safely in hand and had recovered her breath, she turned to Young Tommy again and held out her hand for her mail, asking as she did, "So how is the lane today?"

Young Tommy dutifully handed her the official correspondence addressed to her, keeping back the letter from Mr. Green, as usual, and related the prosaic happenings of the day that had elapsed since last he had stood in the 'room' relating such things. She nodded appreciatively, as always, and thanked him as he left, then turned to her newly arrived letters from her distant family. They wrote to her every day, detailing their lives in as much detail as they could muster, and she always did the same, despite the lack of change in her sedentary existence. Her correspondence, and the man who ferried it to and from her, were two of the few windows to the outside world routinely available to her. Her own return letters from the day before were already safely stowed in Young Tommy's mailbag.

Upon exiting the house with the pink pelican statues, Young Tommy walked down the path alongside the house. This path led to a seemingly random spot along the back fence, which bordered a house outside the lane. Once there, Young Tommy knocked twice softly on the wooden slats, and when the return knocks sounded, he slid Paxton Green's letter to Liola between two of the slats. With a satisfied smile on his face, Young Tommy made his way out front again and set out once more on his route. It was a few houses further that he came to Mrs. Tilly's home. She exchanged a glass of lemonade for her mail, taking the cup back after the mailman had slaked his thirst. This exchange was wordless out of necessity, but was always a warm and friendly one. Once more without a word, Young Tommy set out as Mrs. Tilly set the now empty glass down on her patio table and opened her letter from Paxton Green. Easily the second most enthusiastic gardener of the lane, Mrs. Tilly always looked forward to these letters, as they were usually filled with nothing but praise for her lush flowerbeds teaming with vibrant colors and shapes in daedal patterns that would dazzle even the most analytical mind.

Mrs. Tilly gasped inaudibly in shock and almost dropped the letter as she whirled around to confirm what she had just read. Sure enough, there, amongst an arrangement of daffodils, chrysanthemums, and tulips she had been lovingly cultivating the last few weeks, was a molehill. She had not yet made it to that part of her garden this morning, so was surprised at the mention of it in the letter. Losing no time, Mrs. Tilly dashed to her garden shed to retrieve the mole poison. She would not allow such a beast to blight her art. She was stuffing the poison down the hole when Matthew stopped by her fence and tried to ask her directions. When she made absolutely no acknowledgement, or any movement indicating she had heard him, Matthew repeated his query with exactly the same result. Raising his voice in an attempt to make himself heard, he repeated himself once more.

"She can't hear you, Mister."

Matthew stopped mid-sentence at this pronouncement, and turned to the youngest Murphy boy and Bobby, who were standing behind him and grinning. Looking confused and flustered, he asked, "She can't?"

"No, Mister, she can't hear nobody. She's deaf", Bobby giggled as he informed the stranger to the lane.

"Oh, then perhaps you boys can help me."

"Yeah, maybe. Who you looking for?"

"I don't have a name, just an address. I'm looking for house number 34?"

Both boys gasped loudly and suddenly looked scared. Turning as a pair, they ran away, leaving a startled and confused Matthew standing alone on the sidewalk, behind him the ever industrious Mrs. Tilly still oblivious to his presence. After a minute, Matthew shrugged in puzzlement and continued down the lane. Intently scrutinizing each house as he passed, Matthew boggled as to how anyone on this lane found anything, as none of the houses had visible numbering. This was both confounding and frustrating to him, having never set foot in the lane before today, yet he was determined to find his destination, even if he had to ask everyone he met. The young woman whom he had earlier encountered jogging in the other direction had not stopped at his raised hand, instead high-fiving it as she passed.

Spying an old man working diligently in his yard much like the deaf woman, Matthew took a deep breath and approached his picket fence, clearing his throat and saying, "Excuse me, sir."

"I'm not a sir," the old man replied without looking up from his work.

"I'm sorry?"

"I've never been knighted, so I'm not a sir."

"Oh, well, it's mostly just an expression."

"Well, I'm specifically not a sir."

"Okay...", Matthew was understandably taken aback by the exchange, but seeing no one else around to ask, decided to press on, "Well can you tell me where house number 34 is?"

"No."

Matthew did not know how to respond to this. The old man's tone had not been rude or hostile, yet it had been certain, so Matthew did what he always did in cases where he was at a loss for how to respond, and apologized, "Oh, I'm sorry to have bothered you."

"No, as in I cannot tell you."

"...Is it some sort of se-..."

"I cannot tell you because I do not know."

"Well, if you could tell me any of the houses' numbers, I'm sure I could figure it out from there."

"I do not know the numbers of any of the houses."

"...Not even your own?"

Paxton Green stopped his excavation of the flower bulbs to stretch his aging back as he explained, "They renumbered the whole lane about thirty years ago, only they never got around to telling anyone on the lane what their new number was. I'm sure the younger folks picked it up as they moved in, but I never bothered to investigate, never had a need."

"So how do you know which house is which?"

"By knowing who lives where. I know the people, so I know the homes. Who are you looking for?"

Matthew fumbled with the grey paper denoting his destination for a few moments as he tried to think of how to answer, "Oh, uh... I don't know. All I have is an address."

Paxton looked up at the now glaring mid-morning sun as it beat down unmercifully upon all the earth and those that resided there, thanking it wordlessly for providing the vital power for his plants to grow. Leaning down to resume his task, he stated finally, "Then I can't help you."

Matthew watched the faithful gardener at work for another few minutes, marveling at his simplicity, before continuing down the lane, still searching for someone to ask for help. It was Ella and Ida who he finally found and asked, as they sat on their porch trading barbs about each other's more troublesome relations. He waved to them from the sidewalk, and motioned as if to approach. When they indicated this would be fine, he walked up to their porch, holding the grey piece of paper out in front of him as if in explanation. Stopping in front of the porch, he asked, "I do apologize, but can you direct me to house number 34?"

Ella's jaw dropped slightly in shock, but this went unnoticed as Ida, who had been eating a cookie at that moment, started hacking and coughing and convulsing as she discovered her inability to respire baked goods. As she cleared the evidence of her inadvisable activity with the assistance of her partner, Matthew stood by looking particularly useless and uncomfortable, unsure of what to do. After Ida was breathing air absent of crumbs once more, and had gone inside to get a drink of water to ease her now irritated throat, Ella settled back down into her chair and closed her eyes as she tried to slow her panicked breathing. She had no idea of what life would be like without Ida, and did not want to speculate on the possibility. When Matthew gently cleared his throat, her eyes popped open again as she remembered the man.

Glaring at him, as if to blame his intrusion into their life for the incident, she simply pointed directly across the street and remained coldly silent. Matthew at first took her gesture as simple dismissal, but then, following the direction of her aim, noticed for the first time the house with the dead yard. Looking askance at Ella, who nodded curtly in affirmation, Matthew turned to study the house with the dead yard. A stiff wind picked up just then, and a small eddy of lawn clippings swirled up from one side of the house with the dead yard and sped across the lot, missing it entirely, almost as if by choice, to settle on the lawn on the other side. The yard remained desolate and devoid of any sign of life.

Matthew was drawn to it, not in an attractive way, but no less insistent. It was foreboding, but also bewitching, an island of remorseless and wild desolation in a vibrant sea of cultivation and beauty. Even the sunlight that bathed the lane and each of the lovingly maintained houses that lined the lane seemed to dim and dull as it illuminated the drab and dreary structure that somehow stayed in more or less one piece despite a complete lack of upkeep. Matthew felt a chill that could not be blamed on the warm breezes of the day as he stared listlessly at the house with the dead yard.

Inexorably, as sure as the passage of time itself, Matthew walked toward the house with the dead yard. Each step as reluctant as the last, as an apprehension he had never known before gripped him. The sounds of the cheery neighborhood gradually faded and died in his ears and his vision blurred ever so slightly as he stepped from the sidewalk onto the path leading up to the doorway of the house with the dead yard. Every unrelenting stride was accompanied by a breath, but he could hear neither his own footfalls nor inhalation over the sound of his heart throbbing in his chest. It was not a dread but a fatalistic resign that clouded his mind and guided his movements as he stepped onto the porch and raised his hand to knock on the shabby door. When it swung open slowly before he could touch the wood, he was not surprised, which should have unnerved him. He could not see anything inside through the gloom, which should have worried him. Some inexplicable compulsion was drawing him inside, which should have terrified him.

From across the street, Ella watched with rapt fascination as the stranger stared into the interior of the house with the dead yard then reluctantly entered. She could not see him anymore and the door swung slowly closed. Ella turned to Ida and yawned. The mornings had never really agreed with her, but she still got up at this unreasonable hour to spend more of each day with Ida. Her protracted oscitancy coming to an end, she asked, bemused, "Did Wilber ever find that cat that's been bothering his parakeet at night?"

Ida shrugged, "If he has, he's made no mention of it yet. Of course, he hasn't dropped by yet today, so you can ask him when he does."

"If the universe doesn't end before then, I shall."

Ida stared intently at the house across the street, as she often did, and noted to anyone who happened to be listening, which was of course Ella, "It's curious how no one ever enters or leaves that place."

Ella nodded in agreement, even though her partner was not looking in her direction and would not have seen the gesture. They fell silent once more as they regarded the constant curiosity of their lives with the detachment of experienced observers. This silence was only interrupted an hour later when Wilber Tumbleburry trotted up their path, waving amiably at his favorite neighbors. Motioning toward the tray of ginger snaps he asked by way of expression if it was alright for him to take one, as he always did despite their regular assurances that he did not need to ask. He grabbed a cookie and took a seat on the deck chair that Ida pointed to, settling in for the lengthy gossip session with the couple which they conducted at least once a week. Wilber Tumbleburry was always interested in any new details Ella and Ida could impart on their shared interest, the house with the dead yard, and they always had some tidbit he had missed while either away at the library or sleeping soundly.

They passed the next hour discussing the lack of any new developments of note, and the strange, but not unprecedented, lack of strange sounds in the prior day. They paused in their dialogue to watch Leo Tuttle walking past hurriedly, clutching tightly at a towel wrapped around his left hand. Despite the oddness of the spectacle, this only proved a momentary distraction from their prior topic, as Leo Tuttle was always doing something peculiar or inexplicable. Soon, Leo's passing would be forgotten entirely. Leo continued down the lane, grimacing in pain whenever he stumbled a bit. He only had to go a few more blocks before he reached the bus stop, but in his current circumstances even that short distance seemed immeasurable. He squawked as he was brushed on both sides by small forms dashing past him. He was too startled to even yell at the passing youngest Murphy boy and Bobby, who were giggling as they ran toward Liola's home.

They were shouting and laughing at each other, as if they were running away from the scene of some mischievous prank, which they were, as if they were being chased, which they were, and were fleeing to a safe refuge to wait out the temporary ire of their hapless victim, which they were. They careened wildly around various residents of the lane with little regard for their or the residents' safety, as the young invariably do. Most just grunted or smiled in annoyance or bemusement, but some shouted reproaches at them or tried to reach out and grab them short with no success. When at last they reached Liola's home, they were short on breath, but giggling all the same. They made their way around the pink pelican statues, down the path along the side of the house, around to the back of her house, past the back door that never opened and into the barely discernible hole in her hedgerow.

There was a hollow in the center of the bushes that lined most of the back fence that connected from bush to bush, and here was the favorite hideout of the youngest Murphy boy and Bobby. It was here that they planned their adventures, it was here that they hid their treasures, and it was here, in the hidden hollow, that they sought refuge from the adults who did not care for their childish escapades. The birds and squirrels had long ago ceded the whole hedge to the two boys. This was their refuge and their fortress. The bushes had served duty as a pirate ship, a castle, an underground cavern, a courtroom, a spaceship, and at all times a tunnel into another world that only they could see and visit.

Once secure in their hide-away, the youngest Murphy boy and Bobby chattered away in whispers, lest they be heard by their imagined pursuer, whispers far too loud to be stealthy, but quiet enough that none listening could possibly discern anything meaningful. Not that they discussed anything meaningful to anyone else, as they excitedly retold the events they had just experienced, misremembering and embellishing every detail, until their latest amusement was of the greatest magnitude with the highest of stakes and the fraughtest of perils. The erstwhile neighbor they had forayed against became a terrible dragon whom they had vanquished with a mighty spell, which happened to take the form of a water balloon, atop a high mountain in the forests of suburbia. Even woeful Leo Tuttle was transformed in their retelling into a mighty guardian troll they had deftly flanked as they crossed a rickety bridge spanning a yawning chasm without bottom that still somehow held a fearsome river filled with piranha and lava at the same time.

The boys stopped their narrative dialogue suddenly when they heard a creak and scrape of wood from the fence next to the hedge. There was only silence, as much as there ever is silence in a world filled with birds and insects and squirrels and other varieties of life. The two boys held their breath and listened intently, suddenly wholly convinced that they had been found out and their secret lair was about to be exposed to the world at last. Long moments of tension and worry held them captive, but the sound did not repeat. Finally, when they could hold neither their breath nor their tongues any longer, they burst into a frenetic whispered debate as to what had caused the sound or if they had heard any sound at all. They came to the mutual conclusion that they had imagined it, then subsequently decided that they had hidden long enough and the world outside was safe once more, so they peaked out of their hole in the bush before creeping out into Liola's back yard.

Laughing and chattering once more, the pair dashed around the house, not hearing the boards behind their hideaway creak and scrape once more. Dodging and weaving around the pink pelican statues, the youngest Murphy boy and Bobby almost ran over a now exhausted and bedraggled Jane, but even in her weary state, Jane was deft enough to twist about to allow the passage of the young rapscallions. Pausing to catch her breath, Jane leaned over and grabbed her knees to rest as she watched with a smile the ever rambunctious pair of boys dash off, shouting something about pirates and ninjas as they went. Jane liked the kids on the lane, even if sometimes they were a little troublesome. To her mind, that was just part of the nature of kids. Her short rest over, Jane resumed her relaxed jog home, being a mere few houses away from her house. After her usual multi-hour jog, she was more than ready to take a shower and start her day. Just before she turned down her own path to the house with the pink vinyl siding and burnt umber trim, she noticed Candice from across the street waving at her. Turning and smiling, she returned the wave, shouting so as to be heard, "Morning Candice!"

"Morning, Jane! Could I bother you to stop by today? I've got a chest of drawers I need to move, but can't do it by myself."

"Sure thing, Candice! I'll be over in thirty!"

"Thank you, Jane!" Candice smiled at the younger woman as she disappeared into her house, before turning to find Old Mrs. Habernathy glaring at her from her own porch. Frowning at her perpetually persnickety neighbor, Candice turned and walked back into her house. She did not care for Old Mrs. Habernathy, but she could not imagine any but mosquitoes caring for the old crone. Not for the first time, Candice wondered why some folks found it so hard to be pleasant. Or was it that they purposefully set out in life to be bitter and cold, as if that were some grand achievement? Dismissing the issue from her mind, Candice wandered back into her sitting room and sighed, pondering her own immediate personal problem. The chest of drawers sat on the wrong side of the room, in the perfect spot for a chest of drawers. Looking from the drawers to the other side of the room, at the least suitable spot for a chest of drawers, she contemplated how to momentarily hide the disturbingly pallid stain that was growing outward from the pinprick hole on the wall before Jane came over to help her move the drawers there. She settled on a flattened cardboard box, concluding that she could explain its presence as a buffer so as to not scrape or bump the wall with the chest of drawers as they positioned it. Yes, that made sense, Candice thought. Once she had set the cardboard in place, her mind grew easier, as she could no longer see the execrable stain or the hole it was growing from.

Her mind at ease, Candice almost jumped out of her skin as she heard a crash of glass from the front of her house. Had she made it outside, she would have seen the back of Justin's running form disappear down the block. Justin was a troubled young man, too young to be held directly responsible for his actions but far too old to not know better. Lacking adults who actually cared about his wellbeing, Justin made his own decisions about his upbringing, and these decisions were often less than wise. More often than not, Justin did not run these ideas past either of his parents or his teachers before acting upon them. He got into more trouble than was average for his age, all of which was dismissed or ignored by those who should be guiding his development into adulthood. As Justin ran away from his latest foray into self-parenting, he cursed under his breath. He had thought Candice was not at home, and was not sure if he had been seen throwing the stone. Justin had timed his assault on the house for one of the rare occasions when Old Mrs. Habernathy was taking one of her meals inside and not keenly watching everything that occurred on the lane.

Only briefly cursing his own luck, he quickly turned his malice toward Candice herself, blaming, as was the custom of bullies, his victim for having crossed him earlier that week and thus provoking the assault upon her home. Justin only stopped cursing and running when he realized no one was chasing him. Looking around, he found himself in front of Mrs. Tilly's house. Other than the deaf woman busily working away at her garden with her back turned to him, Justin was alone. Justin watched the happy lady with boredom and disdain. How could anyone be that enthusiastic working in the dirt? What an idiot she must be. Well, she was deaf and dumb, so it made sense she would be content with such mindless activities, he thought. He did not even consider Paxton Green in this conclusion, but he was not watching Paxton Green at the moment. He was watching the idiot deaf woman, and he had just decided he wanted her to not be happy anymore. Keeping his eyes on her to make sure she did not turn around, Justin reached down and grabbed her freshly planted bushes firmly at their bases. Pulling hard, Justin uprooted the plants and tossed them out into the street. Laughing at her lack of reaction, he repeated his action with more of her hard work, rapidly reducing her immaculate cultivation to ruins.

It was only after he had also trampled all her newly bloomed flowers into litter that he grew bored and wandered off. All the while, Mrs. Tilly had been oblivious to the carnage ensuing behind her, humming silently to herself as she lovingly aerated the soil around the delicate arrangement of flowers in front of her. Her plants were a large part of her life, and she cultivated and tended to them as if they were her children. Under her care they thrived and grew into beautiful exemplars. To Mrs. Tilly, the smell and feel of the dirt was one of the most pleasing sensations one could have. Not even the discomfort of age could discourage her from experiencing it whenever the sun was out. Standing and inspecting her work, she nodded in satisfaction and stretched her back. Mrs. Tilly turned to start on the next flowerbed and discovered the destruction strewn about her yard and the street beyond. Her eyes bulging in shock and horror, she opened her mouth and emitted a scream no one heard.

Mrs. Tilly stood there, crying and shrieking in silence for several minutes before the first of her neighbors noticed the distraught woman and the destroyed garden. As if by magic, word of the horrible vandalism spread up and down the lane, and just as quickly, her neighbors converged on the scene of the crime. While Jane and Wilber Tumbleburry did their utmost to calm and comfort the distressed Mrs. Tilly, Paxton Green organized and led a concerted effort to salvage what they could of her uprooted plants and repair the ravaged yard. Even the youngest Murphy boy and Bobby were enlisted as gophers for the adults as the reparations were made. In less than an hour, the yard was restored to a condition that would have been satisfactory to most, a condition that only Mrs. Tilly and Paxton Green would know was less than perfect. By this time, poor Mrs. Tilly had vented her anguish sufficiently that she was able to communicate by way of a translator to the police officers who had arrived to take her statement.

As the impromptu landscaping brigade disbanded, none of them being of any use to the police since none of them had seen what had transpired, Jane remembered her promise to Candice and walked over to Candice's residence. Candice, who had not been part of the restoration effort, did not answer the door when Jane rang her bell. This worried Jane a little, and she turned to look at Old Mrs. Habernathy, asking with a look if the old battle-axe knew what was wrong. For her part, Old Mrs. Habernathy just glared silently at Jane like she had always done since the young woman had moved onto the lane. Turning back to the silent door, Jane tried knocking a few more times before giving up and trying the doorknob. It turned and the door opened, as it was not locked. Jane entered while calling out for Candice, but received no reply. It was only when she was inside that Jane noticed the broken front window, with a large rock-shaped hole in the center and a spider web of cracks radiating out to the edges of the frame.

The window only held her attention for the briefest of moments, until her gaze and concern were drawn first to the prone form of Candice on the living room floor, then to the rock lying just beyond the pool of dried blood forming an almost perfectly circular corona around the head of her friend. The ambulance arrived in record time, twenty minutes too late to be of any use at all. The police cruiser, which had only just left the lane, returned and was joined by several others as the end of the lane was cordoned off and a murder investigation was launched. A chill went up and down the lane and everyone felt a little less safe and serene than they had before. Just as with the vandalized garden, no one had seen anything and the police found nothing of use in questioning the various residents, but they diligently made their way up and down the lane, inquiring at every house but two. For no particular reason, they did not approach Old Mrs. Habernathy, and they did not approach the house with the dead yard.

By the time the police left the lane and all of its distraught residents, the sun was setting, and the houses of the lane lit up for the evening meal. Old Mrs. Habernathy got up as the last light of the day faded away behind the picturesque houses and reentered her house to go to bed. A silence settled on the lane as the beasts of the night came out to make their rounds. The cats started their nocturnal stalking of all the smaller creatures that emerged from their holes and dens to feed upon the vegetation on such bountiful offer. The raccoons emerged from their hiding places to feed upon both the flora and on any of the cats ignorant enough to consider raccoons as prey.

It was in the growing darkness of the night that the youngest Murphy boy and Bobby made their way, far less quietly than they imagined, to their secret hideaway in the hedgerow behind Liola's home. Once safely inside, the boys opened the bags of junk food they had brought with them and gorged themselves on unhealthy snacks as they took turns telling each other ghost stories in loud whispers. Even the bold raccoons gave the hole and its occupants a wide berth, not being quite brave enough to intrude upon the hideout while the boys were in it. They would come back later, after the boys had gone home to sleep, to clean up the scraps discarded by the careless youths. As they swapped stories, the boys inside the hedgerow would occasionally turn on their flashlights, either to find a misplaced bag or toy, or to illustrate their torrid tales. The light show this created would have alerted any nearby adult to the boys' presence, but none were about to observe it, so no one but young Tina, who sat outside the hedgerow just close enough to hear the stories being told inside, knew the boys were there in Liola's back yard.

Young Tina had long wanted to join the youngest Murphy boy and Bobby in their adventures, but had never mustered the courage to ask, and had never been invited, as the pair had no idea of her desire or her existence. So while they adventured all over the neighborhood, they were silently shadowed by the little girl a few years their junior, who had gotten quite good at not being noticed, by practice as well as by natural inclination. Tina's mother had always encouraged her daughter to go out and make friends, but had never thought it necessary to make sure that her daughter actually followed through on her request, and as a result, had no idea that her daughter wandered in the shadows of the other kids, alone and lonely, scared of the rejection she never allowed to happen. Young Tina strained to listen to Bobby relate a particularly frightful tale of pirates and captives being walked to their doom on a plank when she started at a sudden yet faint noise from the fence to the right beyond the boys hiding spot. The story inside the bushes did not pause, as they had not heard the scraping sound. Young Tina's heart beat rapidly as the scraping slowly slid along the wooden fence toward where the boys were hidden. Petrified in terror, young Tina tried to cry out to warn the boys, but no sound escaped her clenched throat. Trembling, she reached up and grasped at her neck, as if to tear a reluctant scream from its unrelenting hold as the soft scraping drew ever nearer the unknowing boys in the bush.

It was almost upon them and Tina started to tear up in frustration and fright.

Just as she thought she might be able to cry out, the scraping stopped, and all young Tina was able to hear in the darkness was the fantastic rambling narrative of bound pirate captives battling sharks and crocodiles while dodging sword thrusts on the plank. When she was able to breathe again, young Tina realized she was shaking in alarm and that she was all alone outside in the dark with who knows what creatures of the night. Sobbing and crying, Tina ran out of Liola's back yard, making for the safety of home and mother. She almost ran out into the street in front of the taxi, but stopped just short as the taxi did likewise, then dodged around the car and continued on her way, rubbing tears from her eyes as she went. The taxi driver waited until he saw the little girl he had almost run over make it safely inside of her house before proceeding down the lane to stop in front of Ella and Ida's house. Ida climbed out with some effort and walked up her path to plop down in her favorite deck chair.

Ida was exhausted. After the extempore gardening in Mrs. Tilly's yard earlier that day, Ida had returned with Ella to their house, only to slip and sprain her ankle on their own porch steps. Ella had been beside herself with worry, but Ida had insisted on going to the doctor by herself, not wanting to endure the overbearing attention of her partner the whole time. Besides, she reasoned, Ella would quickly calm down once she was gone and the injury was out of sight. Ida had been incorrect in her reasoning. The door to their home flew open and a very concerned Ella came rushing out to examine the afflicted ankle, all the while gushing a torrent of consternated admonitions and accusations, as should have been expected by anyone the least bit experienced in relationships. Ida endured these attentions about as well as an injured badger, and the pair were soon arguing about proprieties and improprieties at volumes sufficient to attract the observation of the ever alert Wilber Tumbleburry, who exercised inestimable wisdom by staying inside his own home and not getting involved.

The professor listened long enough to discern that no one was in immediate danger of mortal harm, then returned to the task at hand, which in this case was burning a previously palatable pot-roast. Wilber Tumbleburry was a passable painter, an acceptable agriculturalist, a superior scholar, a lithe linguist, and a crappy cook. Of all the many arts and sciences he had endeavored to master over the many years of his life, Wilber Tumbleburry had utterly failed to make any headway in the culinary arts. Multiple chefs and many more relatives had long ago despaired of Wilber ever getting past the level of a barbarian in the kitchen. He had on no less than a dozen occasions burned water, and on uncountable other occasions rendered perfectly edible ingredients into sickening slop, comestible only by porcine, canine, or rodentine creatures, though many of these turned away from his waste bin in a few of the extreme instances.

The ex-pot-roast of this particular evening joined myriad prior attempts at food in the garbage after a few more frustrated attempts at salvage. As soon as Wilber had closed his kitchen door, a small, recently stray dog, more accurately a puppy, emerged from the bushes where he had been sleeping, the smell of a possible meal having aroused him from his nap. The poor puppy had been on a pleasant car trip with his family when they had stopped at a nearby park to play. Having been overly exuberant in his frolicking, the young pup had chased a butterfly for far too long and for a considerable distance away from both the park and his forlorn family. When the puppy had finally found his way back to the park, the sun had long ago set and the only family he had ever known was gone, as were all of the other humans and animals that had been there earlier in the day.

Since that day, the puppy had been making do with the scraps he found in unsecured waste bins and the occasional fallen fruit from the trees on the lane.

The puppy sniffed several times at the endeavored cooking now cooling in the bin behind Wilber Tumbleburry's house before electing to eat any of it. The puppy had his doubts that this was indeed food, but hunger drove him to take a chance. The bin went over with a loud crash, which startled the puppy. He barely had the chance to snatch up the pot-roast and run away before the kitchen door was opened in investigation. The puppy ran further down the lane, finally finding refuge in the hedgerow around the house where Jane lived, where it tucked into his stolen garbage. He had only had a few bites before he was startled once more, this time by Justin, who was hiding between two of the bushes, crouched down with a pair of binoculars, staring intently at one of the upper windows of the house with the pink vinyl siding and burnt umber trim. The puppy, now defensive of the only meal he had secured in a day, growled menacingly at this new threat, intent on protecting his food from this large shadowy form. Justin cursed at him in a harsh whisper, telling the puppy in a language he did not know to shut up. When the puppy growled again, Justin stood up and kicked the poor animal, who yelped in pain before rapidly retreating up the lane, his attempted meal abandoned in his withdrawal.

Justin swore once more before crouching again, but froze in the act of bringing the binoculars up, not needing them to see the well-lit and angry face of Jane glaring down at him from her now open window. Justin panicked but did not initially move, not sure what to do. He dashed up the lane when Jane barked at him, "Hey, you there!"

Justin's mind worked feverishly, as feverishly as it was possible for Justin's mind to work, as he ran. Mostly it repeated a few choice expletives of alarm over and over, but it was able to also conclude that Jane had seen him quite clearly, and likely would be able to identify him. In the distance, Justin thought he heard a siren. It was an ambulance siren several streets away, but that was entirely lost on the alarmed youth. Stopping for a moment to look around desperately for a place to hide, his attention was drawn almost magnetically to the house with the dead yard. No one ever went there, he thought, and no one would ever think to look for him there, he assumed.

Justin ran over the dead yard, stumbling once on a clump of dried dirt, before reaching the porch and the door to the house with the dead yard. The door stood open, which was unnerving, but Justin did not hesitate, his fear of the authorities and their ire far outweighing the suddenly looming sense of dire threat he was getting from the dark interior of the house with the dead yard. Justin slowed to a walk as he crossed over the threshold, but did not stop. Looking once more over his shoulder at the empty darkness of the lane punctuated by the occasional streetlight, Justin stepped into the gloom and the door shut.

The early rays of the sun the next dawn found Paxton Green on his routine walk around the lane, mentally composing the notes he would later write to his neighbors. As he passed by Miss Tilly's immaculate garden, a garden he himself would be proud to call his own, he nodded in satisfaction to see that she had addressed her mole problem effectively. His letter to her would once more be the routine praise it usually was. Hearing them before seeing them, Paxton clucked at the youngest Murphy boy and Bobby as they dashed down the sidewalk from behind him, chasing some phantasm of their overactive imaginations. While he liked the pair, Paxton wished they would exercise more caution around other pedestrians and the cars that they occasionally dodged around.

For their part, the boys neither noticed nor cared about the gentle admonition of the elderly gardener, entirely caught up in their private game. This Sunday morning, they were on a crusade against a foul beast that they fancied lived under the porch of the Peterson residence, and were on their way over there now to vanquish the evil creature before it could rapaciously devour the lives of more innocents. For this noble purpose, the pair had gotten up extraordinarily early that morning and girded themselves with homemade armor, consisting almost exclusively of sports safety gear, and armed themselves with assorted kitchen tools. Bobby's mother had been alert and strict enough to prohibit cutlery or other potentially damaging utensils from their arsenal, and the boys had reluctantly conceded this victory to the mindful parent. Undaunted, they now rushed toward the fray, hoping to catch their quarry unawares in the primeval hours of the day, unconcerned about alerting it with their eager shouts and laughing or the clattering of their armaments as they ran with abandon through the otherwise quiet lane.

They crashed headlong into a distracted Leo Tuttle as the latter disembarked from the city bus, wearing the same clothes he had worn when departing the lane the day before. Leo Tuttle fell almost in slow motion, both his arms, one in a freshly applied cast, wheeling about every which way in a desperate attempt to regain balance and equilibrium, but these delaying tactics failed to stave off physics and the man toppled to the sidewalk next to the two boys who had caused his unfortunate descent. The boys were already sprawled about, their weapons strewn further ahead. For the briefest of moments, after Leo let out a muffled exhalation upon impact, the disaster scene was silent, then Bobby let out a dull whimper, having landed badly on his elbows, scraping them bloody. The bus's parking brake barked as it engaged and the bus driver, Janet, stepped out and started tutting as she checked all three victims for serious injury. In short order, mothers were called and the boys were hauled off to have their boo-boos cared for and their reckless behaviors scolded. Leo Tuttle, meanwhile, was loaded back onto the bus, which had no other passengers yet this morning, to be delivered back to the hospital he had just departed from to address his bruised ribs and hip and sprained left wrist.

Candice wandered past the scene of carnage minutes after the bus had driven away, oblivious to the accident that had just occurred there, on her way to Liola's house. She had a standing appointment for Sunday morning tea that she had yet to miss in all her time on the lane. Her concerns about the pinprick hole on the wall addressed with Jane's help the night before, her mind was free from the ineffable concern that had been growing all the previous week. She breathed in the clean fresh air of the lane, a freshness marred only by the smell of newly cut grass as all the lane burst into almost simultaneous tumult with the sound of lawn mowers and hedge trimmers. The ritual weekend piety to the arbitrarily proper length of lawns was being observed with an enthusiasm bordering on the religious.

Knocking on Liola's door, Candice was still able to clearly hear a bellowed 'Come in!' emanating from the interior over the cacophony of motorized ceremony around her. Candice let herself in, shutting the door behind her on the clattering disturbance of an otherwise pleasant weekend morning. Entering the 'room', Candice nodded to the already seated Wilber Tumbleburry, who nodded in reply. He was busily trying to cool the cup of earl grey in his left hand by waving his right over the top in a lazy back and forth motion. Liola had her back turned to her guests as she fetched down a particular volume from her overburdened library shelves. Both of her companions waited patiently for her to finish her arduous task. Candice used the time to serve herself some tea and a biscuit before settling down in her favorite rocking chair.

Wilber Tumbleburry busied himself by reading, for what had to be the fiftieth time, the titles of the various tomes that resided on those packed shelves, volumes which by their respective levels of dust indicated how frequently or infrequently they were fetched down. Some of the least loved were almost unreadable for the level of buildup that obscured their printed labels. Liola's library contained such a variety of books on an equally varied array of topics that even Wilber Tumbleburry, as savant and erudite as he was in the sundry spheres of research available to the scholars of the world, was lost as to the nature of many of the subjects addressed by the collection. It was this exhaustive archive and his respect for their owner's unparalleled research capabilities that drew Wilber Tumbleburry to these weekly get-togethers, even if the themes of the discussions rarely addressed any interest of his own.

Her book finally retrieved, Liola took a moment to catch her breath before turning back to her company, greeting Candice with a warm smile. Pausing to take a liberal sip of her own tea, now cold, before opening the book she had just retrieved, Liola mumbled to herself as she turned the pages of the ancient manuscript. The syllables she muttered would have made no sense to her guests even if they had been uttered at an audible volume, as they were partial words from a dead tongue only a few individuals over the last few centuries had known how to properly pronounce. There were not many more who knew how to read the simplest of passages of the language and only a few more beyond that even knew of the existence of the language or the people who had created it so many millennia ago. Liola only spoke in these partial words from the dead tongue of the book she was leafing through because she knew better than to give voice to the words fully formed, lest she give substance to them and life to what the words described.

Wilber strained to hear the sounds Liola was mouthing without any success, his fervent longing for all knowledge overriding his better judgment. Well did he know that the information Liola sometimes accessed was beyond his capacity and came at costs he would never be comfortable paying. This was the same reason he had ages ago ceased asking his host to describe the books upon her shelves labeled in scripts and symbols that he neither recognized nor was comfortable looking at for too long. For her part, Candice studiously ignored the book, preferring to pretend that it simply did not exist. Her usual role in these meetings was to steer the conversation away from such topics, and as she stirred her own tea, she silently cursed the 'professor' for arriving early. Liola finally found the page she had been searching for and went silent as she read the words on the page that only she could. Finally, frowning, Liola sighed and shut the book with a thud. Setting it on the top of the stack of other recently retrieved books that served as a de facto secondary side table, she picked up her tea again, sipping it slowly as she contemplated what she had just read.

Finally, with finality, she set her now empty teacup aside and picked up a biscuit before looking directly at the patiently waiting Wilber, saying before she took a bite, "No."

Wilber nodded slowly and sagely, expecting this answer even if he had hoped for a different one. Sipping his own tea he replied, "Ah well, it was worth asking at least. Thank you for looking."

With that, the conversation turned to other, more tangible and harmless topics, and the trio passed the remainder of the morning discussing the recent events or lack thereof on the lane. Midway through, they were joined by Young Tommy, who was dropping off Liola's weekly grocery shopping as he did every Sunday. After unpacking the goods into their proper places and handing out Paxton Green's letters of the day to the two guests, Young Tommy briefly chatted with the trio before heading back home, his work for the week, both official and unofficial, now complete. As he stepped out onto Liola's front porch, he caught a glimpse of young Tina darting around the corner of the house on her way to the back yard. Chuckling in amusement, Young Tommy set out toward home, reminiscing about the adventures he himself had as a child on the lane.

Young Tommy waved to Bobby's mother, who was supervising her son in their yard, the child weeding the flowerbeds for his punishment. The off-duty postman high-fived a jogging Jane before stopping in to snag a cookie from Ella and Ida. Ida smiled as usual as he walked up their path. She was knitting something with too many angles that Young Tommy was not able to make out. She waved to a pitcher of lemonade to go with the cinnamon sugar cookie. Young Tommy thanked her as he poured himself a glass. He had always liked lemonade, ever since he had sold the traditional summer beverage as a youth on the lane. All of the neighbors had made a point of patronizing his stand, even those who were more than capable of making far better lemonade than he was selling, such as Ella and Ida.

As he ate and drank his socially acceptable sugar conveyances and gossiped with Ida as neighbors are expected to do, Ella wandered out of the house and sat down with a flounce and a sigh. Ida eyed her with some exasperation and asked, "So, is it done?"

"Done?"

"You know what I'm referring to."

"Time and space are but an illusion, one which no human is adequately prepared to comprehend nor contemplate. As such, no action can truly be said to be taken, no result actually accomplished."

"Look, just take the trash out."

Young Tommy valiantly resisted reacting to this exchange, and consumed the remainder of his cookie to appear busy and distracted. Ella, ever the dramatic one, sighed again and got up with what seemed all the effort in the world and went back inside to address her derelict household chore. Shortly afterward, Young Tommy bade his neighbor goodbye and left for home and his own neglected domestic tasks. Ida continued to knit and rock in her chair, looking up occasionally to watch the squirrels and neighborhood cats engage in their eternal turf war up and down the lane. She stopped and fixed her whole attention on the house across the street, the house with the dead yard, when a screeching sound such as has never been made on this earth emanated from the deteriorated building. This new noise was particularly loud and harsh, startling her even after all the years she had been watching the house with the dead yard. Snapping angrily to no one in particular, as no one was present, "That does it!", she put her knitting aside and stood up.

Ida took four steps down her path toward the house with the dead yard before a desperate screech from behind stopped her in her tracks, "Ida! What the hell are you doing?!"

Turning back to her partner, who was standing in the doorway, clutching at the frame with whitened knuckles as if it were holding her up, Ida said with some measure of temper, "I have had it, Ella! I am going over there and I am going to find out what exactly is going on in there!"

"Don't you dare!"

"Why not? Someone has to do it, or it will never stop! The noises, the blight that house is! For all we know, that yard is dead due to some chemicals being made in there or something! Someone has got to confront whoever is in there, why not me?!"

Ella shook as she passionately pleaded, "Because I can't lose you, that's why! That house terrifies me, and I won't let you go inside it! Let someone else take the risk! I won't risk you!"

"Who else? Huh? Who is going to do anything?"

"I don't know, but not you!"

Ida fumed as she tried to come up with a reasonable, logical argument to this less-than-reasonable reason for her to not find out once and for all the nature of the house with the dead yard. Her own emotions were running high, but in the end she acquiesced to the unyielding fear of her partner, choosing Ella's happiness over her own determination and indignation. It did not matter that her own logic on the matter was sound, it did not matter that Ella was being irrational and inordinately hysterical, it did not matter that the noises of the house with the dead yard had perturbed them for decades and the whole lane for as long as anyone could remember, it did not matter at all. None of it mattered. The woman she loved was terrified and needed to be mollified. Ida swore passionately in a quiet enough whisper that no one would ever have been able to hear and then stormed past her partner into their own house. She was capitulating, but she did not have to be happy about it. Ella trembled and tried to calm her breathing as she stared fearfully at the house across the lane, the house that had almost taken her Ida from her, then turned and followed Ida inside.

The cinnamon sugar cookies sat on their plate on the table next to the pitcher of lemonade, inanimate, yet at the same time entirely too tempting to be ignored. A young hand, belonging to a young Tina, reached out timidly to snatch up one of the cookies. Then the little hand, and the little girl it belonged to, retreated from the porch at a velocity only children and small animals can achieve. That she was fleeing from no foe with a prize gladly proffered, free to all who would care to claim it, mattered not at all in the bashful mind of the adolescent. Young Tina still believed she was doing something naughty, and so sought some refuge where she could consume her 'ill-gotten' treasure in safety. She remembered then that the boys' hideout was currently empty, and the boys it belonged to were currently occupied with their punishments. Forgetting entirely the terror she had felt the night before, young Tina decided that the hole in the bushes in the back yard of the house with the pink pelican statues was the perfect place to eat a 'stolen' cookie.

Taking the most circuitous route a child can conjure, young Tina made her way surreptitiously down the lane and into the back yard of her destination. Clambering into the hidey-hole, Tina took a moment to explore and examine this secret sanctum of the boys while she had the chance before she settled down to enjoy her 'illicit' cookie. She had only taken a few bites when she heard the sound. She froze mid-chew, alarmed at the intrusion in her assumed isolation, then heard the sound again. Looking down, between the tightly knit branches and the smattering of leaves that had grown on the bottom of the hedge near the ground, she immediately spied the source of the whimpering she had noticed. There, below the bush, was a small, forlorn looking puppy, looking up at her with the most soulful eyes any pup can turn on a human to elicit sympathy. The charming expression worked its magic instantly on the little girl and she almost dropped the cookie while voicing her adoration in a squeal of glee. Placing the partially devoured cookie in the nook of a branch, she scrambled out of the bushes and lay down so she could peer underneath, meeting the despondent eyes of the puppy with a grin.

Slowly, young Tina coaxed the puppy out of his hiding place, petting him a few times before snatching him up fully in her arms and hugging him delightedly. The puppy, for his part, had little choice in the matter, but had not yet been absent an owner long enough nor been abused by anyone in a way so as to grow distrustful of humans. He returned the little girl's affections by eagerly licking her ear and cheek. Young Tina, all memory of her cookie now gone, unabashedly ran directly home with her new prize, her characteristic hesitation and timorousness forgotten. In her innocent young mind, the puppy was already hers and had already been named Bailey. Her parents' approval was not even a consideration.

The precocious little girl ran past Paxton Green's house without even returning the old man's customary wave and smile, her mind already racing with all of the fun and games she would have with her new four-legged friend. Paxton Green watched her go, taking a few moments to distinguish the squirming object she held so tightly as she ran. Chuckling and mentally wishing the little girl the best of luck convincing her parents to allow her the pet, Paxton returned to his current task, transplanting a selection of tulip bulbs from the bed they had spent the prior winter in to a newly prepared patch to the southwest corner of his yard. As he dug up bulb after bulb, however, Paxton Green's familiar smile turned into a consternated frown. By the time he had dug up the whole crop of bulbs, Paxton Green was as close to open swearing as he had ever been. He did not swear, he never did, but if there were any time he would have, it would have been as he finished digging up the last of the blackened bulbs that were oozing a sickly black-green puss. Bringing one of the dead flower bulbs up to sniff it, he grunted. It smelled of death, and not of the vegetable variety.

Tossing the last corrupted bulb into the bucket with the rest and taking up a fresh clean trowel, Paxton Green turned to the surrounding plants, determined to divine how far this foul desecration had spread into his yard. It was after another hour of effort that he found the perimeter of the poison, though he was still ignorant of the cause or the nature of the malady that had destroyed and infected so many of his precious plants. Now that he knew the center of the epidemic, Paxton fetched a spade from his shed and set about digging down, to see if there was a spring or other such source to the stain welling up from below. He was so intently focused on his rapidly deepening excavation that he did not notice the pair of proselytizers standing on the other side of his fence, attempting to garner his attention. After he failed to acknowledge their third greeting, his back still turned to them as he worked, the pair shrugged and moved on. They had many houses to stop at and many folks still to bother that day.

Anne and Andy, not related, were from a congregation a few miles away from the lane, and they were making their rounds on the lane in an attempt to garner more adherents for their particular brand of beliefs, knocking on door after door, greeting those that answered with a smile and a question, handing them a simple pamphlet full of scant details and leading questions which more often than not ended up in waste-bins or fireplaces. They did their best to appear kindly and neighborly as they openly questioned the existing beliefs of all they encountered. Anne and Andy saw nothing wrong in their behavior, they saw nothing negative about casting doubt into the minds of so many, for Anne and Andy knew the underlying truth of the universe, the one key to all understanding. What they believed was correct and everyone else was wrong. So they pursued their mission with vigor and joy, doing their utmost to spread the knowledge of their unquestionable truth to all whom they encountered, and any inconvenience or uncertainty they might inflict was all in the name of this good cause.

A pleasant smile, a simple question, and a 'have a nice day' to every closing door saw Anne and Andy approaching every house on the lane without any fear in their hearts or doubt in their minds. Not even an empty house would deter them, as they littered a pamphlet upon the welcome mat or slid it into the door frame to await the return of the homeowner. Not even a residence with no signs of habitation or occupation, such as the house with the dead yard, was viewed by the pair with any trepidation. Even if there were no actual inhabitants, their theological litter might still find its way into the hands of the impressionable somehow. Yet, as Anne and Andy stood on the porch of the house with the dead yard and reached forward to tuck the pamphlet between the door and the frame, their smiles wavered. The door had swung open, seemingly of its own volition. Anne and Andy looked inside with consternation, and Andy called out for anyone inside to hear, but no answer was given. The religious propagandists stood there, peering into the darkness, unaware of the multiple pairs of eyes watching them in fascination from several shuttered windows along the lane. They stood there, paralyzed in an existential dread they had not known for a long time. With a primordial terror and doubt their faith had so long hidden, Anne and Andy shook and shivered, and yet still they stepped forward, into the shadows within, deep beyond the door of the house with the dead yard, which swung shut behind them slowly and steadily until it was closed once more.

The eyes behind all the shutters glazed and unfocused, and their owners went back to whatever it was they had been doing before they had decided for some unknown reason to once again stare at that creepy house with the dead yard. Across the street, on the porch of Ella and Ida's house, the couple returned to their conversation with Young Tommy about how remarkable it was that no hawkers or hucksters ever bothered the residents of the lane, like they did so often elsewhere in the world. Ida pointed out that even the religious of any faith never pestered them, not even on weekends when that was such a common behavior on other streets. They were so absorbed in their discussion, comparing notes and trying hard to recall anytime such a door-to-door salesman had been spotted on the lane, that all three of them missed the wave from Jane as she ran by, not that her wave was anything more than perfunctory nor did she notice when they did not return it as they always had in the past.

Jane was deep in thought as she ran, pondering how much brighter her life had become since she had moved onto the lane. She liked all of her neighbors, even the odd or ornery ones, or more accurately especially those, and she loved the effort everyone put into making sure the whole lane looked and felt alive and vibrant. She almost shuddered when she accidentally reminisced about her life before the lane, but she quickly dismissed these thoughts, repressing them as she always did. Those days did not bear dwelling on, no good could come from memories of those times. There were so many more pleasant things she could think about, or even nothing at all would be preferable. So she smiled, the surest self-defense she had, and kept running, concentrating instead on the beauty all about her, each lawn or yard a monument to the cultivated care of its keeper.

The serenity of the sound of her own shoes striking the cement with every stride, the rhythmic swing of her arms from side to side as her body sang forward through the air calmed her soul in a way nothing else ever had. She was simultaneously a part of and absent from every point she passed through, and that transience of motion appealed to her on both a rational and emotional level. She was so peacefully in sync with her surroundings this morning it was a pity when the bird swerved to avoid flying over the dead yard and collided with the side of her head.

She staggered into the street, arms wheeling to keep her balance, eyes closed instinctively to prevent harm, a flurry of feathers and fluttering and claws and cawing overwhelming her senses and better judgment. The bird managed to extricate itself from the jumble that was Jane's face and hair in time to allow Jane to open her eyes and see the car. The car, a taxi to be precise, was being driven by Marshall, who was ferrying Leo Tuttle back from the hospital. With his injured passenger in the back of his cab, the last thing Marshall expected to see appear in front of his cab in the middle of the road was a young woman and a bird in mid-confrontation. Initially at a loss for intelligent thought, Marshall nonetheless snapped into action, or rather reaction, and his foot instinctively repositioned the brake pedal as close to the floor as the laws of physics would allow.

Jane, for one terrified moment, saw the taxi and thought she was about to die, only to be left uninjured, from the taxi but not from the bird, as the car screeched to a halt mere millimeters from her outstretched hands. She exchanged a look of shocked silence with Marshall then stepped to the side of the street to let him pass. He pulled up next to her and stopped, rolling down his window to ask, "Are you ok, ma'am?"

Jane was about to offer the standard social reply that she was fine, but then felt the trickles of blood running down her forehead and cheek. She lifted a hand to touch the wet spots to verify that she was indeed injured. Shaking her head no, she sat down on the curb as she started to feel slightly woozy from both the open wounds and the throbbing from where the bird had impacted her temple. No, she was not okay. Marshall dropped Leo Tuttle off in front of his residence, helping the recently discharged hospital patient out of the back of his cab, then returned to where Jane sat to help her into the back of his cab for a return trip to the hospital.

Leo Tuttle watched the cab as it disappeared from the lane before turning and limping up his own drive and into his home. Leo Tuttle closed his front door to the lane behind him and let out a pent up shudder. He never cared much for the outdoors, preferring the comfort of his house's enclosing walls to any of the communing with nature that the rest of the lane held so dear. He was the only resident on the lane to hire the services of a gardener to carry out the directives passed on from Paxton Green. While he always attempted to appear friendly to his neighbors, Leo secretly dreaded the occasional contact or interaction he was forced by the very nature of suburban life to endure, and only ventured outside when needs necessitated. Even the pleasanter ones like Jane made him anxious.

Refreshed now that he was once again safe inside, Leo walked as quietly as he could down the hall, trying his best not to disturb it. As he passed by its room, he could hear it moving about, but not in any alarming way. Leo Tuttle literally tiptoed past the thick, bolted door and made his way into his kitchen, where he set about preparing its evening meal. His time in the hospital had put him behind schedule, but not such that he was yet in any danger. As he pulled out the massive quantities of ingredients required for its repast, Leo heard a sharp cracking sound from outside the kitchen window. Startled, and greatly fearing that it had somehow gotten loose from the house, Leo whirled about and ran over to the window, pulling it up in one swift movement, so that he could lean out to see what had caused the noise. He only caught a glimpse of the disappearing child, and was not able to tell which of the children of the lane it was, but the sight nevertheless calmed his nerves. Spying children were the least of his concerns.

This particular spying child, being the youngest Murphy boy, was now crouching between two parked cars, terrified of being discovered, either by the extremely strange adult, Leo Tuttle, or by his own parents. Neither possibility was at all to his liking, but it was the latter he feared the more, regardless of the mysterious reputation Leo had developed amongst the neighborhood children. The youngest Murphy boy had slipped quietly out of his own home, while his mother had been distracted with his siblings and his father had been distracted by a particularly alluring bottle of unfinished model ship. The youngest Murphy boy was grounded, but had resolved that such a condition was most unconducive to his obligations as a young child to fit as much entertainment as physically possible into each and every day. Besides, he had to have adventures. If he did not, what else would he tell the twins about the next morning?

After waiting a child's eternity, approximately five minutes, the youngest Murphy boy was certain the coast was clear and ventured forth from between the cars. He turned when Old Mrs. Habernathy clucked at him disapprovingly. Noting who it was admonishing him, he ignored her as he always did and ran across the lane into Candice's back yard. He rarely spent any time in this particular back yard, except for the express purpose of going through it. Candice's back yard was bare and empty, save for some decrepit deck furniture that lacked a deck, and was surrounded by a dilapidated slat board fence. It was this fence that held the youngest Murphy boy's interest, and was the sole recommending feature of Candice's back yard. After initially watching for any sign of movement inside the house it adjoined, he dashed across the empty yard, around the disused patio furniture, to a specific board in the fence. Putting his finger in the open knothole near the base of the board, he pulled and twisted the loose board aside, allowing just enough space for him to crawl through the fence into the adjacent back yard.

This yard, which the youngest Murphy boy had never been able to mentally connect to the house it was behind, was truly one of the great back yards of all time. What once had been a neat and orderly array of hedges and garden beds and terraces, intricately woven together in an ideal arrangement to maximize the length of the walking path among the splendors of nature, had long since fallen into neglect. Due to advanced age, the owner of the house and the yard, had lost the mobility and energy to tend to both his front and back yard with sufficient effort, and had long ago abandoned the miniature park behind his house to the natural order of things. The plants, upon the presentation of such a rarefied opportunity on the lane, had seized upon their new-found freedom and grown to their natural limits, engaging in the eons-old warfare for which they had evolved. They encroached upon and attacked their neighbors, resulting in a miniature jungle of entangled vines and branches. The war had since slowed into a mutual detente of the survivors, each far too resilient to defeat and far too weak to take on their equally stubborn foes. The resulting clash of the chaos of nature above and about the neat and orderly, but often broken, borders the plants had strayed from was a surreal maze that frightened many a child and animal who found their way into the back yard. For the youngest Murphy boy and Bobby, this was a world unto itself, full of adventures and delights their imaginations could rarely better, and even the occasional danger they would flee from, but always return to face once more, often with the same result.

The youngest Murphy boy crept into the back yard as he always did, with the fear and respect due to such a wild and untamed landscape. He wove his way through tangle and bramble, making use of many a hidden path known only to the wild beasts, birds, and boys of the world. He had a goal this day, a goal he often had when faced with the wrath of his parents, the scorn of his older siblings, or any time he found himself playing alone. Upon these rare latter times when Bobby was busy or otherwise kept from their games, the youngest Murphy boy did not return to their secret hideaway amongst the bushes lining Liola's back yard. That was their refuge and their fortress, and he never felt right being there without his best friend. No, when he was alone or seeking to be alone, the youngest Murphy boy had but one particular place to himself, and that was in the back yard of wonders, around the mulberry bush, past the place where the poinsettias had once been planted, a place memorialized by a sun-faded plastic tag in the empty flowerbed, through the brambles that had once been a rosebush, there amongst the roots of the beech tree was a natural hollow where two roots rose and parted and then met again. In this hollow was a wicker basket where none should be. It had not been placed there by the gardener who had long ago planted this beech tree. It had not been there the last few decades as generation after generation of neighborhood children discovered and played in this back yard of wonders. It had not been there until the youngest Murphy boy had brought it from his home, where his mother had handed it to him, when it had been filled with fresh baked muffins and a jar of blackberry jam and a small butter knife and a red and white checkered hand towel.

It was into this hollow that the youngest Murphy boy climbed. He sat on the hard root-filled ground and opened his basket, the muffins long eaten, the jam jar long emptied of jam and refilled with marbles, and picked up his favorite toy from its place amongst his treasures, next to the worn down butter knife and the tattered and stained red and white checkered hand towel. He played by himself for hours on end, there in his secret hollow in the roots of the beech tree in the back yard of wonders, where not even Bobby had ever gone. It was there that he played as he tried to forget the harsh words of his mother from earlier that morning, the unkind chastisements of his father over that matter at the bus stop that had not really been his fault anyway, and it was there that he wished that Bobby had not also been grounded or had found a way to sneak out like he had.

Unbeknownst to the small boy, the hollow in the roots of the beech tree was visible, from a particular angle, through the interceding branches and leaves and vines, to anyone who stood in the right place in the study of the house in front of the back yard of wonders, as Stewart often did. Stewart had never minded the children who found and played in his back yard. He had always considered it a special place, and was happy that even after his neglect had turned it feral, that the flora he had planted still served as a magical destination for the young folk that found their way there. He had always admired youth and those who still had it, and while he never chose to interfere with the children in his back yard, he still kept a watchful eye on their activities, lest any should come to harm. It was in this capacity that he kept vigilant as to the youngest Murphy boy whenever the lad sat alone in the midst of his accidental jungle, occasionally checking as he went about his daily activities that the child was still there and still uninjured as he played alone at the foot of the tree.

"Did you know there's a small child in your back yard?"

Stewart looked up from the sculpture he was putting the finishing touches on, to the waiting courier who happened to be standing in the specific spot that could see the small hollow in the roots of the beech tree, and acknowledged absentmindedly, "Mmmhmmm. He's fine."

The courier, named Richard, had not raised the point as a matter of any real interest, just a curiosity he wanted to make sure his employer was aware of, as anyone would want to be, given the nature of the anomaly. Mostly, Richard was endeavoring, with great success, to not look at the sculpture Stewart was finishing. Richard was not a superstitious man, nor was he prone to negative reactions to the unknown or strange, but something about the angle and curve of the sculpture the old man was crafting disturbed him and made his eyes blur. Trying to maintain professionalism, Richard had been averting his gaze to anything and everything not the sculpture, and it was by this behavior that he had spied the boy in the back yard. Now with something active to watch, he kept his gaze on the playing child until Stewart finished his work and covered the sculpture in protective wrapping. Richard helped Stewart crate up the artwork, and wheeled it out the front door of the house. Signing the receipt pad held out to him, Stewart watched as the courier loaded his package into the back of the van and drove away down the lane, then turned and waved in greeting to Candice, who was nervously skulking about her own front porch, looking about for something small, something sneaky.

Candice waved back distractedly to the neighbor she hardly knew and rarely spoke to, whose name she could not even remember, then returned to her hunt for the creature who had somehow slipped into her house the night before, and was now hiding from her and her irritation somewhere amongst her porch furniture or the bushes beyond. She had shrieked when she first saw the creature scratching at the wallpaper in her sitting room, as if the creature meant to tear a hole in the fabric and the board behind it. She had snatched up the closest snatchable object at hand and had chased the creature around her house with great fervor, shouting at the creature vociferously as she did, until the creature had found her front door standing ajar and escaped to the refuge of the outside world.

Now, as Candice searched so strenuously for the creature where the creature was not, the creature sat calmly in her bushes, the ones along her sidewalk and not her deck railing, and watched her with curiosity. The human woman was livid and altogether hostile, but the creature held neither aspect against her, as the creature had invaded her home. Now, the creature simply waited until she grew bored or frustrated with her activity and retreated indoors before wandering down the sidewalk without any trepidation as if the creature had every right to be there. In the creature's mind, the creature had every right to be anywhere the creature happened to be, but the creature was not aggressive in asserting the creature's rights, rather the creature simply acted as if the creature were normal, but retreated without a fight from anyone or anything that objected with vigor. So far the creature had never had to put up a fight, having a natural knack at avoiding corners and the grasp of pursuers.

When there was nothing objecting to the creature's persistence or presence, as was the current case, the creature made the most of the opportunity. So the creature was currently walking at a casual canter down the sidewalk of the lane, surprising the occasional bird or squirrel who took flight or scampered out of the creature's path upon catching sight of the creature. Once, a small girl holding a small puppy, stepped onto the sidewalk in front of the creature, then stepped back in fright, her small puppy putting up a most fearsome protest at the creature's presence. Deciding the small dog was of no real threat, especially while held so tightly in the arms of the scared little girl, the creature went on without deviation, sparing but a backward glance while continuing down and out of the lane.

Young Tina, who was more startled than scared, and far more concerned for her small puppy, Bailey, let the creature wander off without objection. She kept a firm grip on Bailey, who was trying to wriggle out of her arms without harming her to give the creature chase. Once the creature was far out of sight, Bailey calmed down and started whimpering at her as if to ensure that the little girl who had shown him so much kindness was safe. Young Tina cooed at her pet puppy to assure him that all was well, using her now free hand to pet him affectionately, giggling when he licked at her chin. Her parents, with the usual reluctance of any adults would have to the added responsibility of another mouth in the household, had granted their blessing, knowing that one way or the other the pet would prove a valuable life lesson for their daughter. Tina, oblivious to the eventual tedium of chores she had added to her daily activities, had thanked her mother and father profusely, promising as any child would that she would do anything and everything necessary to maintain her new pet, whether she would or not.

With the inseparability and exuberance of any juvenile new pet owner, young Tina had carted the affectionate puppy all around the neighborhood, introducing him to every adult and child alike that stood still long enough to be drawn into the little girl's new-found enthusiasm. Bailey, after the natural initial hesitation any once abandoned animal feels toward the rest of the species that had so cruelly tossed him adrift in the world, excitedly endeared himself to one and all with the encouragement of his delighted young mistress. Bailey adored young Tina like he had adored his original family, like he had adored his own mother when he was born, and had already transferred his undying loyalty to the child, fully willing and able to protect her from the world even at the cost of his own life, devoted absolutely and without reservation as only a dog could be. To Bailey, young Tina was the world, and everything else was either good or bad as indicated by her.

The puppy dangled somewhat below her arms as young Tina struggled to carry him everywhere, determined not to let the puppy go, even if it burdened her to do so. She half stumbled, half ran up to Bobby's house, eager to introduce her puppy to Bobby and his mother, her usual apprehension about the older boy a thing of the past now that she had her puppy in hand. Shifting the young dog to one hand awkwardly, Tina knocked on the door loudly, being far too short to reach the doorbell with her current burden. She waited with all the patience any child can muster until the door was answered by Bobby's mother, then grinned and held up the puppy for inspection, saying for the dozenth time that day, "Look what I got!"

Bobby's mother smiled at the little girl and obligingly cooed at the young dog in her hands, petting him when he warmed up to her, and complementing the little girl on her acquisition. By this time, Bobby, having grown curious as to the commotion, had arrived and pushed his way into the doorway next to his mother to examine the much admired puppy. He added his own words of praise about Bailey, much to Tina's delight and embarrassment, then turned to his mother and suggested, "She should show the twins!" Bobby's mother was hesitant, not sure of the wisdom of introducing an animal, no matter how docile and clean, to the hospital environment of the twins' room, but looking at the pleadingly excited look on her son's face, and the expression of curiosity on Tina's, she reluctantly agreed, but only under her close supervision.

The trio made their way upstairs, Bobby trying to rush despite the admonitory instructions of his mother, Tina with some hesitation, as she had never met the twins. She was very curious about them and definitely wanted to see them, but had the natural trepidation of the unknown anyone would have in her circumstance, tinged at the same time with a new and powerful protectiveness of Bailey, not wanting the puppy to be set upon by this unknown. They entered the twins' room slowly, with Bobby's mother holding the children back from bursting in. The twins looked at the new arrival and the object in her arms with inquisitiveness, then their mouths fell open in delighted grins and they squealed in unrestrained gaiety when they realized what the little girl held. Tina was at first frightened at this sound and the unusual appearance of the twins, but with Bobby's encouragement and with the mother's assistance, she placed the puppy on the bed between the twins as their mother took each of their hands and helped them pet the small animal. Bailey looked at his owner for approval before relaxing and enjoying the attention from the elated pair in the bed.

After an appropriate amount of time, Bobby and the twins' mother decided the twins had experienced enough stimulation for one day. Not wanting to push their or the puppy's limits of tolerance, she had the young children say their goodbyes to the twins, and, with the puppy safely in his owners arms once more, shuttled Bobby and young Tina out of the room and down into the kitchen. She sat them at the table to enjoy some cookies and continue their play with the puppy before returning upstairs to wash the twins' hands and change their blanket and settle them down for some sleep. Bailey romped and played with the sunlight and shadows flickering across the kitchen floor as young Tina frenziedly related the tale of how she had found and adopted the homeless adolescent dog, all the while matching Bobby cookie for cookie. For some reason, all of her previous hesitancy at engaging with the older boy had been forgotten, and she interacted with Bobby as if she had been doing so all of her young life. Bobby, for his part, treated her as if they had always been close friends.

Bobby's mother returned to the kitchen and busied herself with the obligatory tasks of everyday mothering for an hour as the children ate and played, smiling at their ebullience and innocence. When Tina's mother knocked on the front door looking for her wandering daughter, Bobby's mother invited her in and the two mothers had a pleasant conversation comparing their experiences in parenting and the development of their children. All too soon for either of the children, Tina's mother collected her daughter and her daughter's pet and, after promises of further play in future days, conducted her out of the house and down the lane toward home. They stopped briefly at Terrence's house to pick up a bag of dog toys Terrence had promised young Tina when she had introduced her puppy to the pensioner earlier.

Terrence had spent the morning gathering all of the toys and a pair of food bowls from around his house for Bailey. It had been over ten years since his own faithful mutt had passed away of old age, and he had never had the heart to gather up and discard all of the reminders of his faithful companion. The young puppy and his owner had touched his heart, however, and he had not hesitated in promising the relics of his beloved Rex to the younger pet owner. Each time he retrieved one of the treasured objects, he was filled with memories and tears, each object in turn reviving wonderfully cherished moments of Rex as a young puppy, Rex as an older puppy, Rex as a very old puppy, Rex as a decrepit and ancient puppy reluctantly dying in his owners lap, being soothed into the hereafter by the hands that had fed and loved him his entire life, that same old, warm voice cracking as his eyes closed and the world drifted away for the old dog that still was a puppy at the end. Terrence remembered it all as he collected the toys, and mourned all over again. By the time he had finished, he had a very full bag of gifts for the young girl and her young puppy, and very full eyes.

Handing the bag to Tina's mother, Terrence was letting go of a part of himself, but a part of himself he hoped would be treasured by the recipient, even if they did not know why, even if they treasured it in wholly different ways than he had. Watching the little girl and her mother walking away with his bag of memories, Terrence returned to his slightly emptier house, wandering from room to room, not noticing, but still feeling, the absence that dwelt there now. His wandering was aimless, but somehow it still took him where he needed to go. His wandering found him in his bedroom, found him pulling out the photo albums from his youth that he had happened upon during his search for Rex's toys. It found him in his study, looking up his sister's phone number. It found him calling his sister and recollecting about their childhoods and their childhood pets. His wandering found him packing a bag and putting on his coat and hat and leaving his house of so many long years, locking it against the day of his possible return, and it found him climbing into a waiting taxi and leaving the lane where he had lived for so long. His wandering lost him as he left the lane to find a new adventure.

Night fell with the departing lights of the taxi, darkness swirling about on the wind. One by one the streetlights popped to life along the sidewalks, casting their artificial and harsh illumination upon the cracks in the concrete and the imperfections in the asphalt. Their glow, a colorless hue of stark white, struck harsh shadows behind every object it touched, turning even the most innocent of plants and structures into sinister shapes as the stars and the moon were obscured beyond the dense clouds above.

It was in this semi-darkness that Marshall's taxi drove slowly down the lane, proceeding with a caution appropriate in the lessened visibility. Marshall wove his automobile around the parked cars down the length of the lane until he pulled up in front of Jane's house, the house with the pink vinyl siding and burnt umber trim. Putting his car into park, Marshall got out and opened the door for Jane, who slowly exited with his assistance. She was decorated with a variety of bandages and bruises from her accident earlier that day, and was still slightly woozy and unsteady on her feet from the minor concussion she had received. It was not so severe that the hospital would have wanted to keep her overnight, but still such that she allowed Marshall to help her walk the short distance to her door without any of the normal protest she would have otherwise raised.

Thanking and paying the taxi driver, Jane went inside to her own bed to fall into a most deserved sleep. Marshall, calling it a day, returned to his taxi and left the lane, but as he passed, he gave a searching stare at the house with the dead yard, outlined as it was by the emerging moon, a haunting profile jutting sharply into the sky, silhouetted against the familiar lunar surface. Marshall shuddered as he drove on, watching carefully for wandering children and errant birds as he went.

Jane slept for a far shorter period than she had expected or her injury demanded, her head throbbing vexatiously and her wounds aching as they were expected to do while mending. For a time, she vainly tossed and turned in bed, expecting but never receiving a second slumber no matter how much she needed it. At long last, she gave up in frustration and got up, still in the same clothes she had worn to and from the hospital. She paced about her house, not hungry enough to eat, not thirsty enough to drink, and not in enough pain to take anything to dull the sensations. She paced out of frustration from her lack of sleep, out of annoyance for her mishap earlier that day, and out of a general feeling of unease she could not pinpoint the cause of. It was her pacing that made her realize that the nausea of the concussion was gone, and that activity and movement were no longer stressing her condition. Deciding to attempt to alleviate her stress in her usual manner, against some minor doubts as to the wisdom of such an action, Jane went for a run.

She ran along in the splintered radiance of the moon and the streetlights, her world illustrated in stark light and shadow. She tried to concentrate on her running, but her mind was fuzzy. She tried to think on the usual musings she so often pondered as she ran, but her mind was muddled, and every thought was diffused in the throbbing that suffused all signals from her weary body. It was when the sharp edges of the shadows started bleeding into the puddles of light that she finally stopped, panting and leaning upon her knees, trying to clear her head as well as not fall forward from the sudden dizziness that she found herself grappling with. Perhaps it had not been advisable to attempt to run so soon after her accident. Perhaps she should go back home and try once more to sleep. Perhaps just staying still for a little while would be better than what she was doing now.

Jane's vision cleared enough for her to realize where it was that she had stopped running. She had not made it far from her house before falling victim to her injuries. She was in front of the house with the dead yard. She turned to stare at the imposing visage of the building as it seemed to stare back at her. She shivered at the seemingly sinister silence and solitude of the structure, so forlorn and out of place on the lane. It almost seemed to grow larger the longer she looked at it. It was getting larger, or at least it appeared to be, but it was Jane who was approaching the still structure, stepping slowly across the dead yard until she stood upon its porch, the overshadowing presence of the house towering over her. She did not know why she had stepped onto the porch, she did not know why she had walked up to it at all, she did not know why she did not turn and walk away. The door to the house with the dead yard swung slowly open, yawning without a sound, beckoning without any indication, and Jane numbly entered the darkness inside. Just as slowly as it had opened, the door closed shut, and the latch clicked with a resounding clank that punctuated the silence of the night.

The lane was suddenly full of the typical sounds of night. The wind would occasionally rustle leaves or tap branches against the sides of houses or fences, the cats would sometimes happen upon each other and hiss or even squabble loudly, and the crickets would continue their cacophony from dusk 'til dawn. In all the stillness in-between, there rumbled twice a disturbing sound from the house with the dead yard, heard up and down the lane, cursed by some, noted by others. The sounds were new, as they always were, and disturbed the sleep of many of the residents of the lane. When day dawned once more, the house was once again silent, alone, and inert.

The start of a new week on the lane was a ritual repeated across suburbia no matter the era, as those with regular hourly employment awoke at hours they would prefer not to, engaged in the requisite activities to ready themselves for their time away from home and family, and then set out into the world at large to earn the necessary livings to continue their permanence in their preferred culture. On the lane, a dozen garages opened over the course of an hour and a dozen cars rumbled to life and spirited dozens of the residents of the lane to their places of employment. This routine egress was followed by a brief respite of activity, where the illusion of the serenity of the night briefly reasserted itself in the early hour of the morning, before all of the school aged children were ceremoniously conducted out of their respective houses by their parents, with all of the expected yawning and complaining by both age groups, to stand impatiently in the chill of the departing night before being loaded onto the school bus and shuttled off to their societally-mandated daycare. The parents waved to their departing progeny before returning to their homes to either relax or tend to the younger adolescents who were not yet legally old enough to be sent into the care of strangers on a daily basis.

After this pre-dawn ceremony, the day started off much like it did on any weekend, with Old Mrs. Habernathy parking herself on her porch to watch over the lane, Paxton Green conducting his survey of the horticultural efforts of all of his neighbors, and Young Tommy delivering such daily correspondence as still was conveyed by the antiquated means of paper and ink. Young Tommy smiled, as he did for almost everyone, when he walked up Stewart's drive and handed the express letter to the sculptor, who had been standing there eagerly waiting for the mailman for over an hour, despite the discomfort this caused him. Nodding his thanks absentmindedly to the lane's postman, Stewart took the letter with him back into his house and shut and locked the door before opening the envelope with trembling hands. Inside was the check he expected for his last work, but more importantly, and more worryingly, the envelope also contained the instructions for the next piece his patron was requesting. Stewart read the details with trembling hands and sweat upon his creased brow. He was not nervous about his capability to render the request in stone, he was never worried about that after a lifetime of perfecting his art. He was, however, worried about the unnatural angle and curve demanded, both of which were becoming more unnatural with every request. Stewart had nagging doubts of the ethicality of transforming blank and wholesome stone into such twisted imaginings, but the sums promised increased with each request, and he was in no position to refuse such sums even if he had the moral fortitude to resist, which he did not.

Setting the request document down on his workbench with a sigh, Stewart took up a hammer and a chisel of the appropriate size to start a new piece, and turned to the waiting block of stone. Muttering a heartfelt prayer for forgiveness, he began to inflict deep cuts upon the undeserving stone, fashioning it into a twisted form that he could barely stomach looking at. After the initial round of cuts, he had to take a break and clear his thoughts, so he wandered into his kitchen and made a pot of coffee. As he was returning to his workroom, Stewart glanced out the window into his back yard, more out of habit than any expectation of seeing a child there at this early morning hour, and almost dropped the pot in surprise. There, amongst the roots of the beech tree, nestled in the hollow, slept the youngest Murphy boy. The child should not be there, not this early in the day. Stewart did not remember exactly what outfit the boy had worn the day before, but it seemed the same. The child must have fallen asleep under the tree. Concern for the boy's health, as he had slept outside in the chill of the night, wrestled with a nagging question as to why he had not yet heard that the boy was missing from home. There was, like in most neighborhoods, a means of such news disseminating throughout the lane, usually within minutes of its initiation. But he had not received a call from Ella or Ida, and Wilber Tumbleburry had not yet knocked on his door to inform him of a missing child.

There came a knock at his door just then, as if to emphasize his last thought, and the sound startled Stewart sufficiently that this time the pot did drop, spilling coffee all over his workroom's hardwood floor. Tearing his eyes away from the peacefully dozing child in his back yard, Stewart limped as fast as he could to the front door and opened it to find the very concerned Wilber Tumbleburry he had expected. In short order, the news of the youngest Murphy boy's location was relayed back to the worried parents, who had not noticed their child's absence until the morning meal after his older siblings had been bundled off to school. This was considered somewhat reasonable as the boy had been grounded the previous day, and had last been seen sequestered in his room to serve his punishment. Without being woken, the youngest Murphy boy was retrieved from his natural cradle at the base of the tree and carried back to his home and his room, to be tucked back into bed, and punished after he awoke later that day. In all the unusual excitement, Wilber Tumbleburry had not noticed Young Tommy picking up a letter from the house with the dead yard, well outside the established schedule.

After the errant child had been safely conducted home, and he had exchanged a few thoughts about the matter with Stewart, Wilber Tumbleburry made his way home. He returned to his abandoned book on the topic of ancient omens of antiquated origins for an hour of further reading before wandering across the street to Ella and Ida's house. Ida was sitting on her favorite porch swing, as usual, and the pastry of the day were very appetizing blueberry muffins, which Wilber took great delight in savoring as he related the morning's occurrence to the rapt Ida. Ella joined them after awhile, at her usual untimely hour of awakening, and Wilber necessarily retold the whole narrative for her benefit, not that he minded the repetition in the slightest. They were both attentive and concerned over the whole affair, as would be expected amongst tightly knit communities, and all three made several comments toward the character of a family that could so misplace a child for the whole of a night, none of which would ever be repeated in the presence of the family in question. While it was proper to prate and explicate the proceedings of their fellow residents, it was entirely unbecoming to voice such judgments to the judged.

They were still engaged in this sensational gossip of the Murphy family and all of its recent scandals when they stopped to watch Leo Tuttle staggering down the sidewalk next to the house with the dead yard. Leo was clutching at one of his arms with his opposing hand, and grimacing every time he did. Leo, seemingly aware there were now eyes upon him, stopped his pace and turned his head to observe his observers. Letting go of his troubled arm with a wince, Leo Tuttle forced a tortured smile and waved exaggeratedly to the trio. They waved back mechanically, still startled at his stressed demeanor. Either thinking or pretending that they were sufficiently fooled regarding his welfare, Leo Tuttle turned his head back how it had been before and set out once more, staggering every painful step toward the bus stop. Ella wondered aloud why the fool man did not simply call a taxi or ambulance, but neither her partner nor the professor were still present to hear her observation. Ida had risen from her seat and hurried inside to call for such an ambulance, and Wilber Tumbleburry had left the porch to rush to the distressed man's aide. Upon reaching Leo's side, Wilber noted with a single glance that the arm in question was broken, but not cut. There was no blood yet it was hanging at an unnatural angle. Furthermore, without having to ask, Wilber could tell that Leo's left leg was the one causing the man pain as he walked.

Even though he had already surmised the symptoms that were afflicting Leo Tuttle that morning, Wilber Tumbleburry was unable to keep himself from asking the entirely unnecessary and ridiculous question, "Are you all right?"

Leo nodded, gritting his teeth as he muttered, "I'm fine, thank you."

Wilber knew foolish pride when he saw it, even though he would never be caught dead exhibiting it himself, and interposed himself physically in the other man's path, very effectively stopping the smaller and thinner man. Wilber then said, as if it needed to be said to make it possible for

Leo to admit it, "You are injured! Please, rest here while an ambulance is sent for!"

Leo ground his teeth in frustration at the unwelcome interference that all decent folk seemed incapable of withholding, before nodding reluctantly. He could see by the look in Wilber's determined stare that he would get no further without resistance, even if it entailed being physically restrained. So he sat down on the curb, with Wilber's insistent assistance, and tried not to think too much on the pain that his arm and leg were attempting to overwhelm him with. It was only a matter of twenty minutes before he had been loaded into the back of an ambulance and driven off to the hospital once more. Wilber and Ida stood on the sidewalk in silence as they watched their odd neighbor being driven away. Despite repeated inquiries, neither had gotten a single detail out of Leo as to the cause or extent of his injuries. Ida snapped out of her reverie and looked at her watch, noting the time and letting out a mild curse. Saying goodbye to Wilber, Ida rushed back inside her and Ella's house, ignoring the askance exhibited by Ella as she passed, and emerged once more with a cellophane wrapped plate of cookies, setting off at a hurried pace toward George's house.

As she walked up George's drive toward the house with the pink vinyl siding and burnt umber trim, Ida glanced at the house next door, and noticed that Leo's front door was standing ajar, and resolved to shut it on her way home. While she had never understood or gotten along with Leo Tuttle, Ida held no animosity toward the odd man, and it would be the right thing to do to secure his house until his return. Glancing toward the house beyond Leo's, Ida noted Old Mrs. Habernathy staring at her with her usual withering scorn and quickly turned away. The old crone gave her the shivers. Knocking on the door, Ida waited only a few minutes, during which she tried to formulate some form of acceptable excuse for the absence of Ella, before George answered with a grin. George always had a grin on his face when talking with Ida or Ella, or anyone else Ida had ever seen him interact with. George was pleasant like that.

George took the proffered plate of cookies from her extended hand with a nod and a thank you before saying, "She's not here yet, her plane is running late, but you are welcome to come in to wait. She should only be ten minutes or so now."

Ida chuckled, both at the invitation and at her own rush at being late now rendered unnecessary, "I'd love to wait to meet your daughter! What's another ten minutes, eh?" The two friends laughed, a laughter interrupted by the most ungodly screech from Old Mrs. Habernathy. They turned in unison to see the old lady standing, trembling and clutching the railing of her porch as if she were about to fall over. They would have been concerned for her health, but she was not grasping at her chest or fainting, or exhibiting any other signs that she was in danger. Old Mrs. Habernathy was trembling, but not out of ill health, rather she was trembling in anger as she pointed an accusatory finger at George, her mouth hanging open in aghast unbelief. George almost dropped the plate of cookies out of shock at Old Mrs. Habernathy's glare, but before he could, the old woman had shifted her scowl, and her damning finger from him to some distant point down the lane.

Old Mrs. Habernathy's face snarled into something hideous to behold as she shook her finger at something neither Ida nor George could observe, and she let forth a torrent of outraged syllables in some incomprehensible tongue, each word of which could have set a sailor's ears aflame, had any sailors known what the words were. This torrent of invective continued for some time, and grew louder the longer it went on, and Ida eventually found the courage to venture far enough into the street so that she could see that Old Mrs. Habernathy was pointing at the house with the dead yard. For its own part, the house with the dead yard stood as silent and still as it usually did during the day, absorbing the abuse heaped upon it by the little old lady without any sign of discomfiture. By this point, many of the other residents of the lane had ventured forth from their houses to observe the tirade, each equally curious as to the cause of the sudden outburst of hateful pronouncements from the usually taciturn fixture at the end of the lane.

Ignoring the quizzical concern of her younger neighbors, Old Mrs. Habernathy, now worked up into a proper fury, let go of her porch railing and marched across her own lawn, down the middle of the road, and onto the dead yard, never dropping her condemnatory finger nor ceasing her verbal assault. Old Mrs. Habernathy strode with comminatory deportment up to a few feet from the house with the dead yard, now occasionally punctuating her harangue by spitting vehemently, both at the house and upon the dirt around it where no life grew. In the minds of many of the other residents of the lane, this frenzy was as disturbing as it was unprecedented, though there were a few that watched intrigued. More than one called the hospital, at least one called the police, but none called out to her to ask her reason. At long last, seemingly as without reason as when it started, the paroxysm ceased, and Old Mrs. Habernathy simply stood glaring at the house with the dead yard, letting her hand drop at long last. She was obviously unsatisfied, but was no longer voicing her dissatisfaction. Turning on her heel, she marched just as steadily back to her own house, entering and shutting the door behind her. Old Mrs. Habernathy did not emerge again the rest of the day. When the medical and legal authorities eventually arrived, they took the statements of those who had summoned them, knocked a few times at the old woman's door, and then shrugged and drove away, entirely unconcerned. Within an hour, life upon the lane had returned to the normal activities of a typical weekday, even as many a hushed conversation was held about the incident.

In the tumult surrounding Old Mrs. Habernathy's confrontation with the house with the dead yard, no notice was taken of Amanda's arrival upon the lane, pulling two large suitcases behind her after disembarking from the bus. With a parting wave to the departing Janet, Amanda set out toward her father's house, idly wondering about the police cars and ambulance at some of the other houses, determining to ask her father about them after she settled in and got some rest from her trip. It had been a long flight, made all the less comfortable by her condition, but it had not bothered her beyond the concomitant exhaustion. She was relieved to have arrived at last, excited to be reunited with her beloved father after such a long separation over such a great distance, and sanguine about her future life on the lane. She had not grown up here, but she had heard so much about the lane from her father over the years, and had long ago grown to love this neighborhood she had never actually seen. Arriving at the house with the pink vinyl siding and burnt umber trim, she let go of her luggage leashes and knocked on the door, irrationally nervous all of a sudden. She had only a minute to wait before the door was standing open and her father's loving arms were around her, tears in both of their eyes as they greeted each other as only a parent and child could and all her doubts were forever gone.

They exchanged pleasantries between bursts of emotions and sobbing, with George asking his child about her flight, about her previous life, about the child she was bearing, all while forgetting they were still standing in his doorway and about Ida sitting patiently in his living room waiting to welcome his daughter in turn. After his wits returned and he had conducted his daughter inside, George gathered up her suitcases and reentered their home and closed the door. His daughter was home at last, and he had never been happier.

After a charming evening witnessing the reunion of a father and a long lost daughter, Ida said her goodbyes and exited the home, a smile on her face and a few tears in her eyes. She had known George over ten years now, and knew how much he loved his daughter and how long he had longed for reconciliation. Sniffing back a happy sob, Ida almost did not notice the curtain drawn aside in Old Mrs. Habernathy's front window. Turning to stare in turn at the bitter old woman staring back at her, Ida thought again of the incident earlier in the day, and wondered once more about the neighbor no one knew much about, the neighbor who seemed to watch everyone with the same guarded suspicion and distaste. The grumpy woman's outburst earlier had been by far the most animated or emotional anyone had ever seen her, and even though no one had understood what she had said, the words she had barked at the house with the dead yard had been more than she had ever uttered in the company of anyone else in her entire time on the lane. Ida disliked Old Mrs. Habernathy, even more than most, viewing the elder woman's chronic distemper as a weakness rather than as a reason to fear and respect her as everyone else seemed to. In her experience, Ida had found that a pleasant demeanor was far more rewarding for all involved than sourness, and she estimated that she had just as much respect on the lane with her method as the crone who sat silent vigil over the affairs of the neighborhood.

Pondering this oddity naturally caused Ida to once more ponder the house the revilement had been directed at, the house that stood directly across from her and Ella's house, the house no one ever went into or out of, the house with the dead yard. There had been some rather disturbing sounds from the house last night, which was nothing particularly new, but such noises always troubled her, not the least because they invariably woke her from her light sleep. Ella never had such problems, and only heard the nocturnal disturbances when she was up in the middle of the night for a snack or a rare bout of insomnia. They always woke Ida. As she walked back home, Ida regarded the house with the dead yard for the millionth time, and pondered what could be done to remove this perpetual nuisance from her, and everyone else's, life. In the past, she had attempted to call the authorities when the noises were occurring, but by the time officers arrived to deal with the issue, the noises had invariably abated. Ella had once looked into the ownership of the lot, in an attempt to issue legal grievance, but the lot was without record in the municipality. It was a legal void. All attempts to have it recorded or annexed as a public lot had met with the frustratingly predictable bureaucracy of government. Ida wondered if there was any way to have the place condemned as abandoned without a ten-year waiting period and a legion of lawyers. She made a mental note to look into the matter.

With a deliberate effort, Ida put the house with the dead yard and Old Mrs. Habernathy out of her mind. It was Monday evening, and as always on Monday evenings, Ella and Ida would be expecting company. Jogging over to Leo's house, she shut his still ajar door, not noticing the strange sound that issued from one of the closed rooms inside. Now hurrying, Ida returned home in time to assist a distraught Ella in the usual preparations for dinner. By the time the table was set and the food was nearly ready to serve, there was a loud thumping from their front door. They had tried in the past to explain to their guest about the volume of the summons, but such was in vain, and they had long ago let the contention go. Opening the door, they greeted Mrs. Tilly with the warmth and affection expected of very old friends, peculiar in this case only for the silence it was conducted in. In Mrs. Tilly's presence, Ella and Ida conducted all conversation in sign language in deference to their childhood companion. With a rapid series of hand gestures, the hosts and guest caught each other up on the events of the week as they settled around the table for the evening meal. When Ella brought up Old Mrs. Habernathy's uncharacteristic tirade, despite a reproachful glance from Ida, Mrs. Tilly was equally enthralled and appalled. Such outrageous events, while entertaining in such a quiet neighborhood, were also scandalous, and she commented on how it was simply shocking for such a thing to happen on the lane. Ida did her best to steer the conversation to more socially polite topics, but her love and their friend were not to be deterred from their juicy gossip and expressed character judgments, not when the incident involved the two most notorious oddities of the lane.

When at last the pair grew bored of their prattle, Ella asked Mrs. Tilly about her garden. At this question, a question she never tired of answering at great length, Mrs. Tilly beamed like a happy mother as she related all of her activities of the past week and the plans she had concocted for floral arrangements since they last had dinner. Ida relaxed as the conversation returned to familiar ground, and the remainder of the evening passed with much merriment as all such Monday evenings passed in Ella and Ida's home. When Mrs. Tilly left that night, it was with a full stomach and a cheerful smile. As she strolled down the lane toward her own home with its perfectly appointed lawn and garden still gloriously illuminated even in the light of the moon and the streetlights, she did not see Young Tommy waving to her from his own porch. Young Tommy had also impulsively shouted hello, which she naturally did not hear, and then looked awkwardly around to see if anyone had noticed his folly. No one had, as he seemed to be the only one outside this night other than his deaf neighbor, who vanished into her home without a backward glance.

Turning his gaze once more upon the stars above, Young Tommy returned to counting off the constellations he recognized. There were so many, as Young Tommy had been fascinated by the heavens from an early age, spending many a summer night like he was now, finding patterns among the twinkling lights of the night sky that few others could. Most had lost interest in the sands of the sky in the modern age, either from a lack of need to navigate by the arbitrary positions and arrangements of asterisms and galaxies or from the scarcity of sufficient darkness to make out more than a handful of the majestic markers. Not Young Tommy. Most of his childhood found him upon remote hilltops, worrying his mother as he passed far too many a school night staring up, imagining shapes where none existed, drawing lines upon the firmament to connect vast distances with his fingers and fancy. He had long ago exhausted the constellation charts of many cultures from around the world, and had created his own where none yet stood. Even now, as he grew older and wiser, Young Tommy still spent many a night trying to spy the constructs he had crafted in his childhood through the ever present glow of the lane. He missed his hilltops.

"Whatcha lookin' at, Mister?"

Young Tommy blinked as he looked over to see Bobby and young Tina watching him from the sidewalk a few feet from his porch. Tina's mother was hovering within arm's reach, having stopped their walk to answer a text on her phone. Young Tina was holding a puppy in an awkward way, but the puppy looked like he would rather be nowhere else than in her arms, even occasionally licking her neck affectionately. Bobby had a finger up his nose as he stared at their postman questioningly. Young Tommy grinned at the children and pointed up at the most visible constellation, "You see those stars? That cluster, over there to the north, it's called Draco, or the dragon. Do you see it? There's the head near the horizon, and then it's long curving body, up then down and then up again. Can you see it?"

The children squinted through the dim light of the street at the sky beyond, but they shook their heads. They could not see the shape of a dragon in the seemingly unrelated points of light Young Tommy was indicating. Young Tina's mother, having finished her text, chuckled and knelt down next to the children, trying to guide their eyes to the pattern Young Tommy was trying to get them to imagine, but even with her help, the little girl and boy still could not trace any shape that seemed like a dragon to them. When they got bored and fidgety, Tina's mother and Young Tommy laughed and nodded at each other as she took them in hand and continued their walk to Bobby's house. As they walked, the children giggled and chatted inanely about the stars and the houses they passed and of course as always, they talked about the puppy. Every so often, at rare moments when young Tina slipped back into her previous timidity, it was always the puppy that emboldened her again, ever the distraction from her insecurity.

They trooped up onto Bobby's porch and Bobby let himself in, leaving the door ajar as he ran rowdily to the kitchen, shouting for his mother. When he noticed young Tina and her mother still waiting at the door politely for an invitation to enter, he ran back and grabbed their hands, drawing them in as if they were being silly. Once they were inside, he let go of the adult's hand and enthusiastically pulled young Tina with him as he dashed back toward the kitchen, almost yanking her off her feet in his childish exuberance. Young Tina's mother called out for them to be careful as they went, knowing full well they would pay her no mind. She then turned to greet Bobby's mother who was coming down from the twins' room, drying her hands off on her apron. The twins had just had their evening bath and had been tucked in for the night. The two mothers exchanged warm greetings and a hug, then settled into the comfortable discourse of mothers, recounting the harrowing ordeals they faced daily, empathizing with each other over the minor tragedies that both faced in the course of raising children, sharing concern over the minor uproar the youngest Murphy boy had caused and speculating at the terror the missing child had caused his parents at the discovery of his absence.

Meanwhile, in the kitchen, Bobby and Young Tina were oblivious of the discourse of their parents as they gorged upon the snacks Bobby's mother had set out in anticipation of their return from the park. Each mouthful was consumed around conversation or laughter as they watched the puppy play with his own tail on the floor next to the table. Every so often, with a glance at the door to make sure one of their mothers was not watching, a morsel was hurriedly tossed on the floor as a reward to the playful pup. Whenever the children were not talking about the frolicsome pet, they were recounting their day at the park to each other, laughing and embellishing every tiny detail as if neither had been there and had not participated in the very adventures they were now relating. As is the way with children, they fed upon each other's energy, and as they approached every peak of a particular escapade, their gestures became more animated as the narrative would devolve into breathless half sentences with each interrupting the other to enthusiastically continue the story, until words failed them entirely and they spasmed with laughter. Once they had giggled themselves out, the story of the day at the park would be picked up again, with only the puppy able to disrupt the recital.

At long last, and far too soon for any child, Tina's mother gathered her and her pet to return home, and after the customary lengthy goodbyes and assurances of another outing in the near future, the little girl and her dog were conducted home by her exhausted parent. As the little girl skipped along the sidewalk a short distance ahead of her mother, singing an inane tune she had learned from Bobby, the creature watched her with some curiosity from the bushes. This was the second time the creature had encountered the little girl and her dog, but this time, neither took notice of the creature, hidden as the creature was in the shadows of the night and the branches and leaves of the creature's hiding place. The creature observed the path the humans took, noting which house they eventually entered with a mind to visit their garbage cans later that night. Human children were often fed food that the creature favored, food the children themselves often rejected and the parents subsequently discarded with their rubbish.

The creature waited a few moments to make sure the street was now entirely empty before dropping from the branch of the bush and wandering down the lane toward the only house where food was reliably found. The creature passed by Wilber Tumbleburry's house without a second glance, having long ago realized that the professor produced more ash than edible sustenance. A raccoon wandered out from the professor's cans into the path of the creature before it noticed the creature, leaping a few feet into the air and scrambling back the way it came, screeching in fright. A stray cat saw the creature coming and hissed and spat at the creature while backing itself against a tree, finally turning and climbing up into a lofty refuge. The creature gave no more notice to these animals or any of the other animals that were startled as the creature made a beeline around the side of Old Mrs. Habernathy's house, crawling beneath her back fence through a hole no other animal had ever used. There, in an untended tangle of weeds and brambles, nestled next to thistles and ragweed, were dozens upon dozens of wild okra plants. The owner of the house had not cultivated the delicacy, as she had never once entered her own back yard or given any thought to the plants that grew there, but the plant had thrived there nonetheless, and the creature delighted in this reliable source of a favorite food, spending part of each night amongst the stalks, feasting happily upon the seedpods.

The creature was at last satisfied and wandered back out onto the lane in search of other food, but stopped just short of the sidewalk. There in front of the creature, silhouetted in the moonlight, stood Old Mrs. Habernathy. The creature regarded her with caution, having never encountered her away from her porch and definitely never at night like this. She was not moving, standing stock still, the wind whistling around her raincoat, flapping the edges noisily. She was also not looking at the creature, and eventually the creature realized this and slunk away to the side into Leo Tuttle's bushes. Old Mrs. Habernathy was staring intently at the house with the dead yard, keeping vigil as the night wore on, ignoring the cold and the light rain that came down at midnight, never wavering in the hard winds that battered all of the trees and bushes throughout the long night. She did not blink once, nor did her gaze vacillate, and no animal came down to the end of the lane. The house with the dead yard sat silent, no strange noises exuding in the dark hours. While it remained visibly unchanged, any who would have seen it that night would have sworn it seemed cowed. The dawn found the standoff unabated, Old Mrs. Habernathy was still rooted to the sidewalk in front of her house when Paxton Green set off toward the end of the lane on his morning walk. As he approached her, for the first time in seven decades the dedicated gardener slowed his pace and stopped, confusion and concern breaking through his usual meditative inspection.

He stared at her staring at the house with the dead yard, uncertain if she were even alive, so motionless was her form. After several minutes of uncertainty, Paxton Green did another thing he had never done in the history of the lane, he spoke to Old Mrs. Habernathy, asking, "Are you okay, ma'am?"

She did not answer immediately, nor did she move, and Paxton Green was on the verge of repeating himself when finally, her wizened dry lips cracked ever so slightly and a horrid hiss of a reply escaped, "Leave me be." The hostility in the tone was enough to make even the stout and unflappable Paxton recoil in dismay. He hesitated only a few moments more before shaking his head in disgust at her effrontery and resuming his walk, albeit turning to regard her every few paces, the oddity of the encounter muddling his thoughts for the remainder of his excursion. Young Tommy was the next to try his luck, and if anything, her reply to the poor postman had even more venom than the one before, but the words were the same, and Young Tommy almost yelped in pain before he too hurried off, leaving her once more in her strange standoff against the house with the dead yard. The rest of the day, several brave souls tried their luck, and each was sent off with the same exact phrase. Word spread, both of her unusual activity and that no one should bother her, and the gossip of the day was devoted entirely to what she might possibly be up to and why.

Amanda asked her father what was wrong with the old woman. The incident the day before had already piqued her curiosity and now she was even more mystified by their strange neighbor. George did his best to describe how much of an institution Old Mrs. Habernathy was on the lane, but found he lacked the appropriate words. In the end he had to settle for the less than satisfactory 'She's as much a part of the lane as the lane itself'. This insufficient truism was offered as he left his daughter at home in order to go shopping for groceries. Amanda was still recovering from her trip, and had begged out of the provisioning run when he had asked. All she intended to do that day was recuperate and settle in to her new home, the house with the pink vinyl siding and burnt umber trim. George smiled and nodded and set out in his beat up old car toward the shops in the city. As he drove out of the lane, George waved to Richard, the courier, who was just then entering the lane with a letter. Not needing to transport any large packages or crates on this trip, Richard had opted to ride his bicycle for this delivery.

Stopping just in front of Wilber Tumbleburry's drive, Richard put down the kickstand and walked the rest of the way to the house, glancing with apprehension at the house with the dead yard next door. It struck him that there was something off about that house. He was still glancing over at it distractedly as he handed the letter to Wilber Tumbleburry along with the pad for a signature. Wilber had to repeat himself twice before he turned his attention back to his customer and accepted the pad back with an apology. Wilber, far too distracted by the letter he had been eagerly awaiting, did not notice as Richard once more turned to regard the house with the dead yard with rapt fascination. It was not at all pleasing to look at, and yet it attracted his gaze almost magnetically. All the way back to his bike, he peered at the house with the dead yard, entranced. Richard did not climb on his bicycle to ride back to the office, instead walking the bike along with him as he passed in front of the house with the dead yard. He had not even noticed when he had stopped in front of the house with the dead yard. He was captivated by its visceral allure.

Letting go of his bicycle, Richard unconsciously took a mechanical step toward the house with the dead yard, and then he took another. He was entirely unaware of his motion, not even noticing that the house was now closer, not even when it was looming above him ominously. And then, he was on the porch, reaching for the doorknob, which was already turning of its own accord. Someone cleared their throat very loudly, and Richard snapped his head around to look down the lane. There, at the end of the lane, far away from where he was standing, there was an old woman who looked older than anything, and she was glaring at him. The old woman cleared her throat once more, a ghastly sound that he should not have been able to hear over such a great distance, and Richard jerked back a step. Suddenly, he realized where he was, and found that he was staring far down the lane at an irate Old Mrs. Habernathy. Wondering how he had gotten there, Richard shook his head as if to clear away the cobwebs, and returned to the sidewalk and his waiting bicycle. He could not remember what he had done from when he had stopped in front of Wilber Tumbleburry's house until now, and he had no idea why. He got out his pad to confirm that the delivery had indeed been made before climbing back on his bicycle and leaving the lane.

Richard passed by Young Tommy, who was just turning into Beverly Masterson's drive. Beverly Masterson was not at home at this early hour, as this was a weekday, but Tommy could hear the insistent scratching of her cat, Lady Nincompoop, through the front door as he approached. Kneeling down, Young Tommy lifted the lid of the mail slot to let a paw swipe out of the narrow opening playfully. It paused mid-swing, grasping at the air expectantly. Tommy chuckled and stroked the top of the cat's arm gently, scratching the top of the paw, which flexed and trembled in appreciation as Lady Nincompoop purred inside the door to express her delight. This regular ceremony fulfilled to both participants' satisfaction, the cat withdrew its arm from the mail slot to allow the officially authorized use of the aperture. While he could not see the act, Young Tommy was still able to hear the cat snatch up the letters in her teeth and carry them off to wherever she deposited them for her owner. When Beverly Masterson had described the activity to her postman, he had found it highly amusing, and even now, many years later, it still elicited a bemused giggle to know the cat was exhibiting such a doglike behavior.

Continuing his rounds, he spent a longer than average time in the house with the pink pelican statues, as Liola was in a panic. One of her pipes had burst an hour prior, and her condition had not allowed her to remedy the problem directly. The water had shorted out her telephone's power cord, so even summoning assistance had been beyond her. He had found her trying to drag herself through the pooling water across the kitchen floor to the shutoff valve underneath the sink. Turning off the water had been a trivial matter, but it had taken a little longer to assist her back into her chair. After she was settled in again, Young Tommy spent the next thirty minutes mopping up as much of the water as she would allow him to, using every last towel in her closets. When at last she insisted he get back to work, but not before he had changed out the fuse so her telephone would work again, he left the house with the pink pelican statues, slightly damp and soggy on a cloudless day.

Further down the lane, as he passed by the house with the dead yard, Young Tommy kept glancing at the dilapidated structure with a vague sense of unease. He usually regarded the house warily, but this time, something was different. There was some sense, a sense he could not quite pin down, that something was off, even for the house with the dead yard. Whenever he looked away, he felt as if the vacant dwelling was somehow staring at him, as nonsensical as that notion was, and he kept wanting to look back at the old building. Considering the circumstances, he very much wanted to talk to Wilber Tumbleburry, yet even as Wilber answered his door with a smile, Young Tommy found he could not stop eyeing the professor's 'neighbor'.

Wilber cleared his throat and repeated his greeting. Young Tommy snapped his focus back to the elderly man of books, and blinked. Remembering now why he had stopped here, he related Liola's mishap to one of her dearest friends on the lane. Wilber Tumbleburry, despite his decidedly unathletic physique, managed to reach the end of his own path and was well on his way down the lane toward the house with the pink pelican statues before Young Tommy had taken half a dozen steps back toward the sidewalk. Discussing other folk's affairs without their permission was technically against the rules of his profession, but when it came to matters on the lane, especially with regards to those Young Tommy was close to, he felt no qualms in occasionally disregarding the regulations.

As he watched the rapidly receding back of Wilber Tumbleburry, Young Tommy made his way to the always welcoming front porch of Ella and Ida's home. Ida was uncharacteristically absent, and Ella was likely still in bed inside. The expected plate of confections was present, however. A tall plate of fresh butter cookies sat prominently on the deck table, well protected from wildlife and free floating contaminants by a delicate gossamer silk cloth. The cookies, no more than blurred shapes beneath the covering, advertised their delicious nature and lingering heat with the most delightful odor. There was also a handwritten note on a piece of paper anchored to the table by the plate it accompanied, which demanded of any who read it to 'Eat Me'. After carefully selecting a cookie and re-covering the remainder, Young Tommy glanced around with a smile in expectation of a pitcher containing some refreshing beverage with a corresponding note, but found none.

As he was returning to his route, Young Tommy heard Ella call out from behind. She must have just arisen from slumber, as usual, and seemed unperturbed at her appearance outside in a shift and a bathrobe. She handed Young Tommy a sealed blank envelope and asked him to deliver it personally to Candice. Agreeing without question, Young Tommy took the letter and continued down the lane. Ella watched him go for a moment, then looked around, as if only now realizing she was outside and that it was slightly colder than her clothes were suited for. Shivering slightly and hugging herself, Ella turned and ran back inside. As she was closing the door, she stopped and frowned, glaring with elevated suspicion at the house across the way, the house with the dead yard. How she hated that house, more even than Ida did. Ida disliked the house, but Ella despised it. The ever sinister presence of the creepy structure and its even more perturbing lot without any life was a constant irritant to Ida. To Ella, it was an object of abject terror. To her, it represented everything fearful and wrong in the world, and there was not a day that she did not wish it was gone.

Today, the loathsome abomination that dominated the view from her front porch seemed especially eerie. Ella did not even have to look down the lane to feel the presence of Old Mrs. Habernathy, still standing in front of her own house, still keeping a chilling eye upon the house with the dead yard. Somehow, the old woman's vigil did nothing to comfort Ella, only causing her to be more concerned that something dreadful was in the air, and it involved that accursed structure. Shutting the door slowly, maintaining her own gaze upon the house with the dead yard until the crack of daylight was nothing more than a sliver, Ella unconsciously sighed with relief when at last the latch clicked home and she was able to slump against the wall, exhausted by the strain of being awake and on guard. She knew she should not sleep so much, she knew it bothered Ida, but the comfort and safety of her dreams was ever the alluring temptation, no matter the time of day or night.

She had almost succumbed to the enticement of slumber when Ida returned home. It was a late hour of the morning now, and Ella and Ida spent the remaining time before noon putting away the groceries Ida had returned with, at the same time squabbling about all the normal domestic disputes that arise in the normal course of suburban life. Despite their comfortable life together, Ella and Ida were not immune to the strains and annoyances any couple faced over time, but after so many repetitions of these arguments, their quarrels had become ritualized, and to some degree even their fights had an affection that was undeniable to any who happened to witness them together. Today the most egregious disagreement was that Ida had misunderstood the chicken scratch note indicating they were out of baking soda, and had instead purchased baking powder, of which they still had an ample supply. Ida blamed Ella's lack of penmanship and Ella despaired of anyone who could have read as much of her writing as Ida had and still not be able to decipher her intent.

The spat continued long enough so as to become contentious, yet when the knock at the door came it was dropped and forgotten as easily as if it had never occurred. The pair walked over to the door to answer it together, Ella seemingly oblivious that she was still in a shift and a bathrobe. They greeted Stewart with a warm smile. The sculptor had made a habit of dropping by uninvited for the sole purpose of handing them overflowing baskets of fruit from the handful of overproducing trees in his side yard, one of the few of his previously grandiose gardening endeavors he still had any time or energy to maintain. He kept large wicker baskets below the trees to catch their fruit, then picked through what fell for those in good shape to hand out to his neighbors throughout the harvest season. No one minded in the slightest that the baskets kept getting smaller and smaller as the years wore on. The basket he handed Ida today held a variety of apples and pears, interspersed with a few late season plums and a handful of early oranges. He also offered a small container of mulberries. As they accepted these gifts and thanked him as profusely as always, they also had to assure him they did not mind the unusual absence of strawberries and tomatoes this year. Stewart explained he had been forced to abandon his ground crops due to his bad back, and that he had not had the time this year to plant tomatoes.

While Ida was once more tempted to explain to him the illogic of apologizing for not being able to give freely what he had once in the past been able to, Ella simply smiled and hugged him, which silenced his explanations far more effectively. Ella knew that no one wanted to be told that it was alright to not be generous, and no one wanted to be reminded that their age was an adequate explanation of their increasing incapacity at the things they once found so enjoyable and once had an abundance of energy and time for. Thanking the elderly sculptor and gardener again, Ella asked if he would be interested in some tea and muffins, a fresh batch of blueberry muffins having only just been pulled from the oven. He perked up at the notion, but then remembering that he was behind on his current commission, begged off staying any longer. At their insistence, he still left with a cloth bundle of half a dozen fresh hot muffins to take back with him to his home studio.

Walking to his house with as close to a skip in his step as his years would allow, Stewart idly sniffed at his recently acquired muffins, appreciating the sweet smell with a smile. While he generally favored savory foods, like many on the lane he had a soft spot for baked goods, especially those originating in the oven of Ella and Ida. He had not mentioned it at the time they gave him the muffins, but he had already eaten one of the butter cookies before knocking on their door to give them the fruit. Not that they would have minded in the slightest, but he still felt slightly guilty about it. As he turned into his own drive, he noticed a chastened child, the youngest Murphy boy, standing on his porch, trying very hard to not look up at him as he approached. Beside and behind the reluctant youth stood his mother, who had a firm grip on his shoulder and the determined look every parent wears when they are doing their best to be the responsible adult they think themselves to be.

Stewart sighed silently, knowing full well what was coming and the role he was expected to play in the ritual, but not relishing the upcoming ordeal. He reached his own porch, where the child and his mother awaited him, and stopped, greeting the youngest Murphy boy with an appropriately neutral, "Hello."

The boy looked up reluctantly, and seemed at a loss for words until his mother tightened her grip on his shoulder, prompting him to start his prepared apology, "Hello... I want to apologize for yesterday. I should not have trespassed in your back yard. It's wrong to go on someone else's property without their permission. I'm very sorry that I did it." The brief speech took forever for the young boy to stumble through, especially the larger words, each of which his mother had to prompt him with when he came to them. The whole time the youngest Murphy boy kept flinching away from eye contact with Stewart, uncomfortable in the steady gaze of the old man.

Stewart wanted to assure the boy that it was alright, that he did not mind if he played in his back yard, that the boy or any other child was welcome to have adventures among the plants he himself could no longer enjoy in his advancing years, but Stewart knew that such assurances would be counterproductive to the lesson the boy's mother was trying to teach him, and would not be taken kindly by this parent, or any other. So instead, he nodded his head gravely and answered in a serious, but not upset tone, "Thank you for apologizing, young man. It was the right thing for you to do. Hopefully, you learn from this and are more mindful of your actions and respectful of others in the future." The youngest Murphy boy nodded his head as if he was taking all this to heart, though it was far more likely he simply wanted to disappear entirely from embarrassment and shame and was doing whatever he thought would hasten the end of the whole encounter. The boy's mother was smiling with satisfaction at how the proper things were being said, and nodded respectfully to Stewart, squeezing her son's shoulder one last time to prompt a mumbled 'thank you' before guiding him back toward the sidewalk and on toward home.

Stewart was about to open his door and enter when he sighed and stopped. Turning back to the retreating forms, he said, "And make sure you ask me next time you want to play in my back yard!" The youngest Murphy boy turned and grinned before looking up and noticing the mildly upset look on his mother's face.

Masking his renewed joy with his best attempt at a serious expression, the boy nodded a little too eagerly to acknowledge the sanction masked as an admonition. His mother nodded again at the elderly sculptor, this time with a slightly perturbed expression. Then she once more turned her son toward home, steering him along the sidewalk with her hand on his shoulder, as if to prevent him from darting from her control at any moment. They stopped briefly at Bobby's house so the mothers could coordinate the exact terms and conditions of the punishments being administered for the recent misdeeds. While they were in council, Bobby managed to whisper the news about young Tina's puppy to his friend, and they excitedly communicated in the semi-secret code they had developed over the years a tentative plan for escape from their mothers' watch and a rendezvous later on.

When the youngest Murphy boy and his mother left, Bobby turned to his own mother and with doe-like eyes, begged to be allowed to fetch cookies from Ella and Ida's for the twins. Bobby's mother was a bit of a light touch when it came to her son, and her recent resolve, bolstered by the encouragement of another parent, melted under her son's charms. While she still wanted very much for him to adopt more caution in his play and habits, she could not convince herself that her son had done altogether too much harm in the incident at the bus stop. After extracting an entirely unconvincing promise from Bobby to not play with the youngest Murphy boy until told otherwise, she released Bobby from his bondage, on a temporary basis, allowing him to leave the house for the express purpose of fetching the aforementioned cookies, and nothing else. She smiled ruefully as her son dashed outside laughing. He was a bit of a rapscallion, but he was also a kind and generous boy. He would come back with the cookies, she was certain, but not before a few unrelated adventures.

Bobby made a beeline for the house with the pink pelican statues. He knew that Stewart's magical jungle was off limits for now, at least until some time had passed so that the parents could forget it existed, but he was very certain that only he and his friends knew about the hideaway in the hedge. Giggling to himself at a volume that reached any within earshot, Bobby ran as fast as he could directly toward the secret base, confident that no adult was wise enough to figure out such a clandestine refuge. However, along the way Bobby remembered something that made him alter his course radically, bypassing Liola's house entirely as he barreled past Mrs. Tilly's house with a wave and past Paxton Green's house with a laugh and a shout, past George who was out walking his dog, and to a small spit of land that had no house and, in the mind of the small boy, no owner.

Bobby reached the spit of land and ducked behind one of the bushes that separated it from the sidewalk, as if to hide from a phantom pursuer, the same pursuer most children pretend to be running from whenever they want to play hide and seek with the world. Looking up and down the lane, peaceful in the warm midday sun, Bobby could not see anyone about. Most of the parents were off at work, the older children were back in school, and the remaining residents were either indoors or hard at work tending their gardens and shrubberies. He was safe. He had never been in danger, but now he was safe from the prying eyes of older, more responsible humans, who would likely stop him from digging holes in the vacant lot that did not belong to his family. Turning his back on the street and giving it no more attention, after all once he was safe he would be safe until he next thought to check, Bobby paced out the specific number of steps he and the youngest Murphy boy had used to demarcate the location of their secret 'pirate' treasure when they had buried it here ages ago last week. The boys had many treasures stashed away in many locations around the lane, but this was their 'pirate' treasure, a small collection of their most prized possessions.

Observed by none but the birds and the bugs, Bobby made short work of the foot of dirt concealing their prized treasure from the clutches of all the other children and the meddlesome adults of the world. Once he had uncovered the small tin box, discolored from its time in the earth, Bobby opened the lid and took account of the small horde he and his best friend had amassed over the last few months. There was the novelty magnifying glass the youngest Murphy boy had won in a knot tying competition at summer camp, which they had made extensive use of to catalogue every last bug that had been unfortunate enough to wander into their presence. After Bobby accidentally stepped on it, the cracked piece of plastic had been deemed a prized relic, and had been placed into their treasure box.

Beside it lay the small metal toy car Bobby had gotten on his birthday, the one the boys had built a launch platform for, the one which they had propelled off of the platform with the force of one hundred tightly wound rubber bands, the one that had soared with tremendous force through Bobby's bedroom window and through the window of their neighbor, Beverly Masterson, the one that ended its epic flight embedded in the cracked and aged oil portrait of Beverly's beloved grandfather. It had taken two hours every school day after Beverly got home from teaching and three hours every Saturday working in Beverly's yard as well as both boys' allowances for the next three months to make the matter right with the preschool teacher. In the end, they not only got their precious toy car back, but also endeared themselves to the wronged teacher and her demented cat, Lady Nincompoop. They had been given an open invitation to visit her whenever they felt like it, but after their long servitude to pay off their damages, the boys rarely felt any desire to visit their onetime place of bondage unless given proper motivation. When they did return, it was usually to say hello to Lady Nincompoop.

Bobby picked up the car and looked it over carefully, as if he did not already know every contour, every dent, and every missing patch of paint by heart, before placing it back in the box with the care one would show a fine piece of china. Ignoring the mesh bag of marbles that they had placed in the tin box after having given up on finding anything remotely entertaining about them, imagining that their presence in their treasure chest might impart some value to the playthings of a bygone era, Bobby picked up the small felt pouch beside the marble bag. The once luxurious pale pink pouch had developed a decidedly putrid green tinge as the moisture of the surrounding dirt had seeped into the tin container and had caused mold to breed in the wool. Bobby did not notice the presence of this contaminant, and pried apart the knot that held the sack closed, dropping its contents into his awaiting hand. Unlike the various childhood treasures that dwelt in the box, this was an item of real value, and would have delighted any adult who might have found it.

Bobby studied the gold coin with the same care and diligence as he had studied the damaged toy car, but the centuries old coin from a long ago fallen empire had few flaws and very little wear. The boys had found it the year before while they had been exploring the basement of Thaddeus Rush. The octogenarian had passed away in his sleep one winter evening and had not been discovered for a month. The death had been the gossip on the lane for weeks, but after no heirs had been found for his estate, the house sat vacant and boarded up for several more months while the courts searched for any distant relation to inherit the old man's mortal goods. The house had not sat in probate for long before Bobby and the youngest Murphy boy braved where few dared, and found a broken window with a loose board that gave them access into the basement. From that day forward their adventures found them exploring the dusty boxes and worn chests that held untold treasures and surprises under the vacant house. Of all the strange and wonderful items the boys discovered while trespassing amongst the cobwebs and mice, their favorite was a small glass case set into one of the walls, a glass case that locked with an antique key.

There was only one item in this case, a small gold coin with strange and fascinating symbols and words that neither boy understood as they marveled at the tiny metal disk through the glass. Every day they were in the basement, they would always spend a few minutes staring at the coin and imagining where it came from and what it meant to the old man who had owned it. Sadly for the boys, nothing lasts forever, and at long last the courts ruled that the estate of Thaddeus Rush would escheat. It was reasoned that no one would want to live in the house where the body of the old man had lain for a month, so the grand old house was to be torn down and the lot would then be sold to a local developer. When news of the decision resparked the interest of the lane, Bobby and the youngest Murphy boy planned one last adventure in the basement before the house was cleared out in the coming days. They spent the time well, playing with their favorite unknown objects, imagining each to be an artifact of tremendous value or power in their games. When at last the time came to go home and bid the basement of wonders a fond farewell, the youngest Murphy boy lingered behind, staying a little longer than his friend.

Looking at the coin and recalling their adventures in the basement fondly, Bobby remembered when the coin had magically appeared in the tin box the next time he had looked inside. Putting it back in its protective moldy bag, Bobby placed it delicately in its proper spot in the box and grinned. Of all their treasures, the coin was his favorite. But he was not here for the coin, he had not dug up their treasure chest for the car or the marbles or the magnifying glass, or any of a dozen other, less remarkable items the boys had placed in the tin container during their many adventures. He was here for the collar with the dog tag. They had found it in the trash. A few weeks ago, a garbage truck had broken down on the lane. While the driver waited for a tow truck, the boys had snuck up to the open back of the truck to examine the refuse within. They had not expected to find anything of value, but they were unable to resist the lure of the unknown the opportunity had presented. They had held their noses against the putrid odors as they rooted amongst the discards of dozens of other neighborhoods, mostly mangled together from the hydraulic press of the truck.

It had been Bobby who had spotted the dog collar, partially embedded in a half-empty takeout container, but it had been the youngest Murphy boy who reached in and retrieved the soggy accessory from the trash. While not adverse to filth, being young boys, they could smell altogether too well, and so washed the collar as best they could before stowing it in their treasure chest. It was made of fine leather and the shiny silver tag that dangled from the ring on the front read 'Bailey'. The first time young Tina had told him the name of her new puppy, Bobby knew that it had been fate that they had found this collar, and that he must give it to the little girl for her pet. Grinning triumphantly, Bobby snatched it out of the tin box and pocketed it for later. Noticing the position of the sun in the sky and remembering his plans for the rest of the day, Bobby hurriedly reburied the box in the empty lot then ran the rest of the way to the house with the pink pelican statues.

As the young boy dashed noisily around the corner of her house, Liola watched him through the window with a mournful smile. She remembered being that young. She remembered what life had been like at that age, the imagination, the anxious energy, the days that seemed to never end. She also remembered the pain she had felt watching all of the other children run about and play with such wild abandon as she cried from her room, sitting in her wheelchair. She had tried playing with the other children, but all too soon they grew weary of the limits she could not help but inflict upon their activities. One by one, they drifted away and stopped coming by and asking her to play, and every day she grew more lonely and miserable. Her mother had been little help, but then, her mother had never cared for her disabled daughter and the encumbrances such a daughter placed upon her social activities. When the other children had drifted away, Liola's mother had seemed relieved, no longer needing to explain her daughter's embarrassing condition to the other parents. It was simply easier to not resist the growing solitude of the poor child.

It was only through the love of her father, Bradley, that Liola emerged from her childhood with any happiness. Bradley despised the reactions of others to his daughter and many were the righteous rages of furious anger he felt toward those who had shown her affection, only to discard her when it became an inconvenience to care. Liola had been the light of his life, and he would have gone to any lengths to make her happy. Long were the hours he spent with his daughter, valiantly attempting to be the friend she needed at all times. Liola's hand rested on the worn leather cover of the book that was always on the table next to her chair. She had read the book a dozen times at least after her father had first placed it in her excited hands, going back to it time and time again even after her father procured hundreds of other books for her enjoyment. She had memorized the book, each word a cherished gift from her beloved father. Even though she had not read the book since the day her father had died so long ago, she still remembered every word. It had not been moved from the side table since she had settled into her current living conditions, yet it had never gotten dusty. Whenever she thought of her father, she would stroke the cover of the book, wearing the leather down a little bit each time. The leather was paper-thin now.

"Are you alright, Liola?"

Drawing in her breath suddenly and deeply, as if broken from a trance, Liola blinked back some unnoticed tears at the fond memories of her dearly departed father, and turned her attention from the window to one of her closest friends in this life, answering, "Yes, I am fine, Wilber. You really shouldn't make such a fuss over me. You go to far too much trouble."

Wilber was holding an armful of soaked towels he had been using to mop up the remainder of the water mess from that morning, his usually tidy clothes the worse for wear from the morning's manual labor. He was disheveled and sweating, not normally accustomed to such feats or lengths of physical exertion, but he also wore a smile that a hundred such days of toil could not possibly have shifted from his face. It was a patient and kind smile, one that he had perfected over the years of his friendship with the irascible and stubborn chair-bound woman he so admired. With the forbearance that only a true friend could show to the foibles of their companions, Wilber deposited the load of wet towels in the basket next to his usual chair and settled down in it for a respite and admonished his close friend, "When will you realize that there is no trouble that friends will not go to when the need arises? To be sure, I have put you to far more 'trouble' in the many years I have known you, often bothering you for some seemingly useless bit of trivia. This... this is but a trifle in life, an inconsequentiality. Not to be thought of again."

Before Liola could object further, or sigh in exasperation at the pomposity of Wilber's language, there came a set of footsteps along her path that she could distinctly identify, and she called out her usual greeting, "Come on in, Candice!" Despite his assurances to the contrary, Liola felt a tremendous debt to the 'professor' for all his efforts to clean up the aftermath of the broken pipe, and was grateful for the interruption by her other true friend. Candice came bursting in with a deeply concerned expression, which changed instantaneously to one of resentful frustration that Wilber had come to Liola's aide long before she had gotten the chance to learn of the crisis. Candice felt protective of Liola, and while she knew that Wilber held no danger to their disabled companion, she did not trust the dabbler of knowledge. She only tolerated him for Liola's sake. He had far too many questions that seemed far better left unasked, and Liola was always one to seek out the answers.

Wilber Tumbleburry, far from being the naive academic he often appeared to be, was highly attentive to moods and mannerisms, and quickly deduced that his presence was rapidly growing unwelcome. Rather than resenting the almost palpable yet unearned animus from Candice or the distress Liola was radiating at his generosity, Wilber smiled and bowed to the women and let himself out, making a quick excuse about a prior engagement. He held no resentment because he understood far better than most the motivations and emotions of mankind. If there was any one subject he would consider himself an actual bona fide expert in, it was the human condition. It was this understanding that granted him a unique empathy few have ever mastered. Once outside of the house, standing next to the pink pelican statues, he paused a moment to rearrange his shirt and sweater, so as to look slightly less bedraggled than he felt. He may not have been an adherent of high fashion, but Wilber still had some modicum of pride in his outward appearance.

As he retied his bow tie, Wilber studied one of the pink pelican statues that festooned Liola's front yard like a beacon of bad taste. These were no ordinary plastic ornaments, being cast out of a heavy and hardy cement that was dyed rather than painted. They had withstood the weather of the years with little to show for the efforts of the elements to wear them away. He tried to recall the circumstances of their arrival, as they had not always been in her front yard. It seemed to his memory that one day the yard had stood relatively empty, notwithstanding the well groomed garden that was obligatory for houses on the lane, and the next, there were a half dozen of the pink pelican statues dotted around the remaining empty spaces of the lawn. Actually, now that he was concentrating on his first memory of seeing them, he was finding it difficult to recall precisely how many had first appeared. It seemed that it was fewer at first than there were now, but by how many he just could not recollect. It seemed a trivial matter, and most would have dismissed it as such without a second thought, but Wilber thrived on trivial matters, and had a mind honed for the monumental tasks involved with devoting oneself wholeheartedly to extracting every last exacting detail, even if there had been no such details before his examination. Such trifles of information often led to greater, weightier mysteries, and this particular riddle was no different, as Wilber had already struck upon the greater question of how the yard of his friend, who was physically incapable of such labors, was maintained, and maintained to the same levels of excellence as the others on the lane. He knew Candice had not undertaken the chore, and he himself had never touched the yard with the pink pelican statues and so far had not given the matter any thought. Now, he had a fresh puzzle to ponder, and it was this development more than anything else that day that brought a smile to his face.

Not wanting to tarry in Liola's yard any longer lest he give the lie to his reason for leaving, Wilber made a quick, yet painstaking, survey of the number and position of the statues as they now stood, mentally logging the information for when he arrived home so that he could document it in detail. This done, he strode down the lane toward Paxton Green's yard. He had a few questions for the wise old gardener that few other mortal men would have the expertise to adequately answer. Particularly, he was seeking advice on how much water to give to his own petunias, and at which times of the day and week would best be suited for the task. Walking along with a skip in his step that should have been impossible for a man his age after the unexpected work in Liola's house, Wilber whistled a nameless tune he had found in an ancient text years ago, enjoying the moments when his melody matched the songs of the birds in the trees and air around him.

Wilber waved cheerfully, as he always did, at the three excited children chasing a small puppy. They giggled and laughed, not at the adult they did not notice as they passed, but at the delighted barks and yelps of Bailey as the young dog raced them home to Tina's house. Wilber chuckled at their youthful recreation, reminiscing fondly on his own youth spent adventuring in kind through the tales and deeds spun from the pages of his favorite books. To Wilber, there was no difference between the real world and the world of the words that had suffused his childhood imagination with endless delight. Even when he knew what he was reading was a falsehood, he imagined that in some way it was still true, if only in the mental constructs of those reading the words.

His current mental construct, which was an interweaving of all of the various fantastical phantasmal exploits of his childhood self and the recent mundane happenings on the lane, was shattered by the clearing of a throat behind him. Closing his eyes as he tried to commit to memory one of the more poignant epiphanies from the vision, Wilber Tumbleburry turned with a smile to engage with another of his neighbors. It was Leo Tuttle. He was wearing a cast, as was to be expected. He was also carrying a saber, which was not at all expected. Wilber restrained his surprise at the object's presence on the lane, especially in the hands of the otherwise mild-mannered nebbish in front of him. However, since Leo was not holding the sword in a threatening manner, rather holding it gingerly as if in fear that the blade would leap up and bite him, Wilber did not at all feel threatened by the weapon and was able to maintain his good cheer as he greeted Leo, "Good to see you back from the hospital! You are looking much better."

Leo opened his mouth as if to reply, then shut it with a frown. Leo did not know how to respond to the man's lack of concern for the weapon he held. He had expected some sort of reaction to it, any sort of reaction to it. When none came, Leo suddenly had no idea what to say. He took a minute to recompose his thoughts, a minute Wilber cheerfully gave him, not at all off-put by the silence. Remembering why he had approached the professor, Leo said, "I wanted to... thank you... for helping me earlier. I should not have... been short with you... about the matter."

Wilber brushed aside the man's gratitude, much to Leo's annoyance and relief, "Think nothing of it! It was just what neighbors do. You would have done the same for me."

Leo squinted at the genial scholar, noticing for the first time his uncharacteristic unkempt state, trying to determine if the man was mocking him or was genuinely that optimistic about the nature of other human beings. Concluding that there was no more genuine human over the age of puberty than Wilber Tumbleburry, Leo grunted and nodded in agreement, then glanced nervously down at the sheathless saber he held at his side. Wilber must have followed Leo's eyes and known that the man wanted to broach the topic of the blade but did not know how to bring it up. Wilber did the only polite thing to do in such circumstances. Wilber pointedly ignored the sword entirely. Excusing himself, Wilber continued down the lane toward Paxton Green's yard a short distance away.

Leo watched him go, incredulous and annoyed. He had wanted to be questioned about the saber. He had deliberately sought out Wilber on his way back from the store explicitly so as to be confronted about the sword. Perhaps, he thought, if he had been able to adequately explain the saber to the professor, to explain why he had it and why he had to use it, he could justify it to himself at the same time. But the exasperating little intellectual had frustrated his attempts and dismissed something that should have demanded his attention without a second glance. It was infuriating. Leo blinked and looked down at his hand, noticing that as he had been ruminating on the perceived affront his hand had been tightening its grip on the handle of the saber. Relaxing slightly, Leo watched with apprehension as the color drained back into his whitened knuckles. Perhaps, he thought, perhaps the saber was not the correct solution. Perhaps there was another, less extreme, resolution that needed to be explored. Perhaps Wilber had rebutted his unspoken reasoning without saying a word.

Nodding his head in thanks to the absent back of his erstwhile neighbor, Leo turned and limped home, resolving to return the sword in the morning. He would find a different answer to his conundrum. As the afternoon sun began to approach the tops of the trees across from his house, Leo once more hesitated at his own front door. He had to take several measured breaths to regain his confidence before entering his own home, where it was waiting for him. He almost lost his resolve not to use the saber. He was startled out of his daze by a woman's voice, and he glanced over in time to see his neighbors, George and Amanda, wave hello to him as they were leaving the house with the pink vinyl siding and burnt umber trim to go for a stroll to the park.

Amanda was zipping up her jacket against the slight chill of the departing sun as her father locked their front door. They both smiled and waved to Leo as he jerked his head hurriedly in recognition before ducking into his house. George could not be sure, but he thought Leo had been trying to hide something long and shiny behind him. Shrugging at the always eccentric behavior of their odd next door neighbor, George turned to his daughter with a smile, "Ready?"

Amanda took a deep breath of the fragrant air of the lane, perfumed by the tens of thousands of different exotic varieties of plants that decorated the yards and gardens along the small street, and returned her father's smile, "Yeah, let's go!"

Amanda looped her arm in her father's, as much for support from her father in this new and apprehensive chapter of her life as to reassure him that she was still there, that she was not going to disappear again, that he would not be left alone, that she loved him. Arm in arm, they strolled casually down the lane, stopping every so often so Amanda could examine some of the more elaborate floral arrangements and topiaries of their neighbors. She oohed and awed appreciatively at the creativity and passion on display. As her father introduced her to her new home and she met more and more of the people who had done the work, she expressed her admiration for their dedication to such a laborious hobby. George beamed as his daughter met his friends on the lane and made new friends of her own. He even learned something new about his daughter when she started signing to a delighted Mrs. Tilly and the pair of them held an extensive conversation that delayed the remainder of their walk by an hour. The whole time they discussed whatever it was that they discussed, George just smiled as he watched, unbidden tears of pride flowing as he became acquainted with the fine young woman his daughter had become. He had not dreamed he could be this happy, not for a very long time.

Mrs. Tilly shooed the nice young lady and her doting father away when she noticed the expectant mother was growing physically weary of standing in one place for as long as she had, wishing her well on her walk and inviting her back whenever she pleased. Elated to have found a new friend, especially one who could converse with her directly, Mrs. Tilly wiped away a stray tear and turned back to the rose bush she was planting. She was not yet ready to unpot the new crop of lilacs this year, so the rose bush was the last of her planned tasks for the front yard that day. After she had settled the bush in the prepared hole and watered it the appropriate amount, Mrs. Tilly made a cursory circuit of her front yard, inspecting her beloved plants for any signs of disease or insect infestation, as well as keeping a diligent eye out for encroaching weeds.

Smiling in satisfaction at the condition and appearance of her front yard, Mrs. Tilly refilled her watering bucket in her kitchen before entering her back yard. Of all of the back yards on the lane, it was one of the smallest, yet even here she had managed to cram more variety of flora than anyone but Paxton Green and perhaps Stewart before the elderly sculptor had let his go wild. Humming soundlessly to herself as she tended to her rhododendrons and her hydrangeas, she was incapable of appreciating how gratingly out of tune she would have been had she been emitting any sound at all. Not possessing the faculty of hearing anything, she found joy instead in the vibrations in her throat, and so the tune was chaotic and painful to the ear of any dog unfortunate enough to listen. The bees that hovered and darted around her busy hands as they worked amongst the branches and stems of the bushes paid her and her cacophonous supersonic intonations no mind. The hummingbirds that swarmed around her head, like expectant children waiting impatiently for their mother's attention, seemed as deaf as the little lady to the impossible sound, perhaps even drawn to it instinctively after so many years spent in the care of Mrs. Tilly.

As the hours wore away above her and the afternoon heat was broken by the shadow of her own house, Mrs. Tilly fed the insatiable birds that dwelt year round in her back yard. Once they were happily at work emptying the dozen feeders hanging from her trees, Mrs. Tilly took a break from her gardening to sit in the lone chair standing in her yard. It was one of the most uncomfortable chairs ever built by man, outside of those designed to keep students awake in classrooms, and it looked at any moment as if it were going to collapse. Originally cast in iron, the passage of time and the persistence of the rains had altered the chair in such a way that it seemed to have been cast entirely of rust. Every week, Mrs. Tilly would have to change out the cloth cover she kept on it, not wanting the rust to stain her clothes when she sat on it. Having placed a fresh new cover on the chair only yesterday, Mrs. Tilly simply settled onto the chair today, sighing and catching her breath from her bustling activities.

Folding her hands in her lap, Mrs. Tilly opened her mouth and silence tumbled forth as she poured out all of her thoughts and dreams, all of her worries and cares, all of the things she had done from the day before until now. She talked without making a sound, sitting upon the uncomfortable chair alone in her back yard, and Mr. Tilly answered without a sound, laying as he ever had, still and unmoving in the grave in front of the chair. It was a conversation the couple had every day, the words coming in a torrent as Mrs. Tilly confided in the one and only love she had ever had in life, and her one true confidant listened as he always had, with undivided attention. There was no holding back, as there had never been a need to hold back from the man she had loved, still loved, and in one tremendous rush of words only she could hear and emotions only he would have understood, Mrs. Tilly let go of all of her anxieties of the day. When at last all of the words had been mouthed and all of the tears had flowed, once more she was at peace with the world. Once more, she was content. She stood up from the least comfortable chair in the world, her husband's favorite piece of furniture in life, and entered her kitchen for a drink of water.

After her refreshment, she bustled about the house, tending to the variety of chores that are never done, only maintained, when she passed by the front door and noticed her. Young Tina was standing outside her screen door, holding up her puppy Bailey, and waving to Mrs. Tilly with one of his paws. Young Tina had missed Mrs. Tilly on her previous rounds through the neighborhood, and wanted to make certain that the kind old woman had a chance to properly appreciate her prized pet, just like everybody else. She had been waiting patiently at the front door for a few minutes, knowing Mrs. Tilly would not hear her knocking, and not daring to simply let herself in. Mrs. Tilly whistled a friendly noise in greeting. It was a noise that had befriended strangers and wild animals alike, a noise she had employed throughout her lifetime without ever once hearing it herself.

Letting the little girl, and her little dog Bailey too, inside, Mrs. Tilly fawned over the dog appropriately for a few minutes before conducting them into her kitchen, where she served the little girl cocoa and biscuits and the puppy a bowl of milk. Young Tina knew very few of the signs that Mrs. Tilly used to talk to others, but struggled to remember the ones her mother had taught her. Her host took the opportunity to teach her a few more, including the sign for dog, before sending them on their way. Tina promised herself, as she lacked the vocabulary to promise Mrs. Tilly, to visit the little old lady who could not talk or hear more often in the future. A block away from Mrs. Tilly's yard, the little girl paused and looked up and down the lane at all of the pretty houses that lined its edges, mentally counting off which ones she had already visited, not wanting to miss the opportunity to endear her pet to any of them, except, of course, the house with the dead yard. She shuddered slightly and looked past the eerie house when her eyes flickered near it, not wanting to see the house with the dead yard, not wanting to think about the house with the dead yard, not wanting to believe in the house with the dead yard.

Her eyes came to rest on the bizarre apparition that was Old Mrs. Habernathy, standing stock still on the sidewalk outside of her house, the only other house that lacked a manicured lawn or many of the other usual signs of maintenance and care that modern suburban life found so fashionable. The old woman did not move as the wind picked up around her, only her long unkempt hair and the ends of her shawl and dress gave any indication that the laws of this world held any sway at all upon Old Mrs. Habernathy, bending and swaying only slightly while the leaves and branches of all the nearby plants whipped about fiercely. Young Tina shivered as the gust reached her and attempted to pick her off her feet, but the shiver was not from the warm summer wind. Tina had never liked the old lady, no child ever had. Never was a smile shown or kind word given by the wrinkled old crone to any living thing, but children had always received her fiercest scowls. Young Tina was only able to look away from the ancient woman when Bailey whimpered in her arms, and she looked down and relaxed her tightening grip on her precious puppy.

Reassuring her pup that all was well, she turned away from Old Mrs. Habernathy with one final shudder, no longer wanting to give the creepy adult any more thought. Suddenly wondering if the boys were available for fun and games, she set out at her default speed of too fast to be safe, running toward the house with the pink pelican statues. She only tripped and fell once on her way there. Bailey, having gotten used to this sort of accident by now, barely yelped in protest as he became a pillow in the ensuing impact. Getting back up as quickly as she had fallen, she let the dog run beside her for once as they took off again for the children's secret rendezvous hide-away. With wild joy and abandon, the pair of juveniles, canine and human, lost themselves in the summer afternoon, their laughter and barking punctuating the buzz of the flying insects and the other ambient noises of modern life.

As they ran toward the house with the pink pelican statues, the pair passed Candice, who was returning home from the very same house. Candice did not even notice the little girl and her dog as she walked slowly down the sidewalk in a haze of frustration and exhaustion. She had spent the last few hours in a furious argument with her dear friend Liola, trying unsuccessfully to convince her that it was unsafe to live alone as she did, given both her condition and the ill-suited design of her habitat in the case of emergencies. All of Candice's suggestions had only served to anger Liola further, yet still she had persisted in her contentions that Liola would best be suited to live with a companion of some kind, preferably human. At first she had proposed that Liola move in with her, but at Liola's umbrage at the mere intimation of leaving her childhood home, the home her father had done his best to adjust to the needs of his beloved daughter, Candice had altered her recommendation to her living with Liola instead. This offer had done little to quell Liola's growing agitation, and after exhausting all of the logic and emotion she could summon, Candice had given up persuading her friend of the necessity of a housemate. Their parting words had been in anger, and Candice had left Liola fuming in her chair, screaming at the empty room of books.

Candice was in a preoccupied state, turning the just ended altercation over and over again in her mind, rephrasing her contentions and reasoning in ways that would never be expressed to anyone but her anger. So distracted was she by this internal torment that she was oblivious to where she was walking. It was only the very sharp and piercing sound of a throat being cleared from several blocks away that stopped her in her tracks, a few paces from the yawning open door of the house with the dead yard. Candice blinked, startled at first simply by the sharp noise that had snapped her concentration from the ethereal back to the real, but then she was startled by where she was, and what was in front of her. She had one foot on the porch of the sinister structure, and the door, of its own accord had opened invitingly to her. Straining, she tried to peer into the gloom of the interior, but could see nothing but darkness beyond the door, in seeming defiance to the laws of nature and the afternoon sun.

A throat was cleared quite loudly once again, and Candice's attention was suddenly drawn to her position once more. She was a foot away from the door frame now, and had just been about to step inside to get a better look into the shadows beyond. She shivered and closed her eyes. The shadows disappeared behind her eyelids and their enticing allure evaporated. Turning around with her eyes firmly closed, Candice strode off the porch of the house with the dead yard before she opened them again. She did not notice the door closing behind her. Candice looked around for the source of the sound that had stopped her twice, but could see no one but Old Mrs. Habernathy, far down the lane, standing like a statue in front of her own dilapidated house. Shaking her head at the notion of hearing the old lady from this far away, Candice dismissed the sound as her own subconscious speaking to her, reaching out to wake her from her own folly, and strode resolutely home. As she approached her own house, she stole glances at her next door neighbor, but the old lady did not give her any of her trademark scowls or glares, her steady gaze forward never wavering, still keeping a resolute vigil against who knows what.

Once more in the safety of her own home, Candice breathed a sigh of relief for some inexplicable reason. Her passionate argument with Liola had somehow vanished from her thoughts, not to return for several hours, and all she could think about was her neighbor and the creepy house her neighbor was still staring at. Stealing a glance between her blinds, she watched her neighbor covertly for a few minutes, wondering how she stayed so still, how she stayed so motionless, even as the winds whipped up all around her and the leaves and litter that infest every city and suburb danced around her in a swirl of motion and light. Growing bored of watching someone who was doing nothing, no matter how strange the circumstance, Candice let the blinds click back into place and went into her kitchen to make a cup of tea. She realized she felt a chill and a cup of hot water and stimulants struck her as the ideal means to alleviate the cold. Digging her teapot out of the cupboard where it had gotten buried behind a thick stack of handwritten notes on ancient languages, Candice rinsed it out and filled it with water, frowning at the slight brownish tinge in the water. The taste of metal had gotten to be unmistakable in her food and drink, such that she could smell it from the water as she set the pot on the stove to heat. She would need to call a plumber to replace some of her aging copper pipes.

As the antique stove did its work, clicking and pinging in protest all the while, Candice rooted around in her cabinets for the box of tea bags she could have sworn she still had there. Quickly, every available surface in her kitchen that was not being heated was covered by stacks of papers and books, all filled with scribbled notes or bookmarks. Some she lay aside with great caution, some she simply tossed wherever she happened to look, though her reasoning for such would have made little sense to any observer. Seemingly ancient tomes, held together by tradition more than their rotted bindings, were treated no better than the cheap notebooks, while what would appear to be random papers she had scrawled some ancient symbol or pictograph upon were handled as if it would strike her down if she mistreated it.

At long last, Candice had ransacked every last nook and cranny in her kitchen and still had not managed to produce the sought after tea bags. Standing amongst her assembled research, she scanned the mess as she contemplated where the tea she knew she possessed had gotten to. Her tea pot was hissing and screaming away and the air was quickly filling with steam, but she did not notice. At last, she smiled as she remembered where she had put the tea. Going to her sitting room, Candice opened the top drawer of her chest of drawers, uttering a triumphant exclamation as finally she saw the errant box of tea bags. Reaching out to pick it up, she immediately snatched her hand back and cried out. Behind the box of tea bags, as well as underneath, was the pallid stain. In a panic, Candice slammed the drawer shut and staggered backward. The stain had spread from the wall behind, creeping into her chest of drawers. This was bad. She had tried to hide it, but it had not stopped. She had tried to not think about it, but still it had seeped further from the microscopic hole in her wall.

She was shaking now, in terror of what this might mean. At last, the shrill sound of her stove cooking off the water in her pot made it through to her mind, and she took the opportunity to distract herself once more from her looming problem. She turned off the heat and took the teapot off the burner. Candice realized she would have to do the one thing she had not wanted to do. There was no helping it, she would not be able to fix this on her own. She would not be able to stop the insidious stain nor reverse the damage already done, not alone. Candice would need to ask Liola for assistance. She swore softly, but realized it was the only option, the only choice she could make. Fortunately, she knew Liola would help her without hesitation. Their most recent dispute would not matter in the slightest.

Her course of action decided, she wasted no time in setting out toward Liola's house, her tea long forgotten. Candice was so distracted by her mission to solicit Liola's aide that she almost ran over Ella, stopping just short of colliding with the smaller woman. Ella, visibly flustered and on the verge of tears, was clutching at the sides of her dressing gown to shield out the strong summer winds. She had been on her way to fetch Candice, and she grabbed at Candice's arms pleadingly, begging, "Come quick, please! We need your help! Ida has fallen! I think she's broken her leg!"

Long neglected instincts clicked into place in Candice's brain, and her training came flooding back. It had been over a decade since she had practiced medicine, but she had not forgotten a thing. Her own pressing errand momentarily postponed, Candice opted to help her distraught neighbor instead. Adopting a soothing tone she had honed from many years at her practice, Candice tried to calm Ella as they marched as quickly as they could to Ella and Ida's house. They stopped just short of the drive to the house. Their path blocked by the creature, which was consuming a discarded apple core from the gutter. Innate fear seized at Candice, freezing her movements as she watched the unnatural movements of the creature on the sidewalk. Ella, her mind clouded with frantic anguish for Ida, only hesitated for a moment. Striding up to the creature, she unleashed all of her irritation in a swift sharp kick, sending the creature sprawling a few feet further down the sidewalk.

Not waiting for the creature to recover, Ella grabbed Candice's hand, ignoring the doctor's shock, dragging her up the path and into the house. The creature, which was still stunned, blinked and coughed, finally dislodging and spitting out half an apple core. The creature had not liked choking.

The experience had been unpleasant and unwelcome. Filled with an indescribable rage toward an unknown assailant, the creature made a sound that scared every pet and wild animal within earshot, setting off a din of animal noises usually heard only at night. The creature was not usually prone to anger, but the anger that was now expressed as the creature stalked down the lane, seeking something or someone to unleash upon, was fearsome and terrifying. A few animals of the slower variety found they could move far faster than they ever before imagined as they spotted the creature advancing in rage in their general direction and fled from the lane. Nothing that could see or hear the creature stayed still.

Mrs. Tilly was kneeling in her garden, as usual, with her back to the street, adjusting the trim and edge of the grass in her lawn with a small set of hand clippers and a trowel. The creature spotted her small form and altered its course, heading right for her. The creature did not care who this woman was or what she had or had not done. The creature wanted revenge for the offence done and the pain felt, and the creature would have that revenge from this woman. Mrs. Tilly was humming as silently as she ever did, as off key as ever, paying no mind to the world around her, outside of her beloved plants, never knowing the dreadful approach of the creature behind her or the harm that would be visited upon her. The creature was seeing nothing but red as it drew closer, tensing up to strike at the vulnerable backside of the deaf woman. Jaws open, snarling viciously, the creature was just about to lunge forward when Paxton Green stepped between them. The creature stopped, ceasing all forward movement in a clatter and scraping of claws upon concrete.

Paxton Green glared down at the creature, armed with nothing more than his hoe and an expression that would have halted armies in ancient times. Without a word, Paxton

Green motioned sharply with his chin, and the creature retreated down the lane and into the bushes around another house. Paxton watched those bushes intently for several minutes before he relaxed his grip and his expression. He would have to set some traps tonight. Turning back toward his own home, Paxton tried to recall the appropriate bait for the creature. Mrs. Tilly continued her enthusiastic gardening, oblivious to what had transpired behind her. Paxton closed the gate to his own yard just in time to prevent Bailey from running head first into it. The puppy was paying more attention to the three children chasing him down the lane than to where he was going, turning every so often to make sure it did not get too far ahead of his mistress and her two friends. They were pretending to pursue a runaway monster, on a rampage through the city, a role Bailey was all too eager to play.

With giggles and shouts, young Tina led the chase, Bobby and the youngest Murphy boy keeping stride behind her, laughing with joy. The three friends had met up in the secret hedge hidey-hole, and after the usual babbled greetings, Bobby had given Tina the collar with the dog tag. Tina had been thrilled and delighted, giving both boys a hug of thanks before fastening the stout little leather collar around Bailey's neck. The puppy, for his part, was a little less enthusiastic about his new adornment, not caring for the initial feeling of entrapment when it was put on. He had nipped and growled at the tag whenever it flashed in his vision, swatting at it with his paws, much to the amusement of his mistress and her friends. When Bailey had noticed how much this entertained Tina, it became a playful game instead of a serious attempt to dislodge the encumbrance. Bailey had danced in circles and yipped and grabbed at the shiny tag with his mouth, going ever faster the more the children laughed at his antics.

Now, as Bailey raced down the lane with young Tina and the boys in hot pursuit, he delighted in the sound the tag made, jingling and jangling with every stride. Whenever the puppy noticed he had gotten too far beyond its mistress, he stopped and waited, wagging his tail excitedly. Tina laughed as she caught up to the puppy, only to have him dash away again, occasionally darting across one of the neighborhood lawns in a playful attempt to lose his pursuers. Bobby and the youngest Murphy boy shouted encouragement and boasted that they would catch the dog before Tina, making her chase her dog ever faster. Tina playfully called out for Bailey to stop, but her tone was not serious enough to halt the puppy, nor was it meant to be. She was enjoying the game as much as the dog was.

"Bailey, stop!", she giggled, as she stumbled on a clod of dirt as the playful pup veered from the sidewalk across another yard.

"Bailey! Stop!", she screamed as she dashed even faster after her puppy, in earnest this time, suddenly all too aware of which yard they were running across. Her beloved Bailey was heading straight for the yawning open door of the house with the dead yard. Behind her, the boys were also screaming at the young dog. Bailey seemed not to hear any of them. Tina was only a few paces behind her puppy as he scrambled onto the porch. Young Tina, tears streaming down her cheeks now, was screeching at her pet to stop as she followed him toward the shadowy interior of the house with the dead yard.

"Tina!"

The sharp bark of an old woman's voice cut through her terror and young Tina froze mid-stride, her forward momentum carrying her off her feet to land roughly on the worn path, just short of the porch of the house with the dead yard. As she winced in pain, she heard a door slam shut in front of her. Young Tina was a little dazed. She turned over and sat up. She had a few minor scrapes on her hands and knees, and she had torn her dress a little in the fall. Blinking, she looked up at the looming, ominous house in front of her, and squeaked. She was in front of the house with the dead yard. She was terrified of this house, why was she sitting in front of it? Why was she this close to the sinister structure, a building that all the children, and some of the adults, of the lane had nightmares about?

A firm and bony hand snatched her up sharply and Tina was suddenly on her feet, staring up in fear at Old Mrs. Habernathy, who was not looking at her even as she held the girl by her collar. Tina was almost as terrified of the old crone as she was of the house, and Old Mrs. Habernathy was not only closer, but touching her. Young Tina tried to shrink into herself and disappear. She was so confused and frightened. She had no idea why she was out here, in the open, and not hiding somewhere safe as she usually was. She had never felt so exposed, so vulnerable. She started to cry. She wanted to run away. Old Mrs. Habernathy never shifted her hateful gaze from the house with the dead yard as she let go of young Tina's shirt and commanded imperiously, "Go home, Tina."

Young Tina fled from the old woman, the house with the dead yard, and the eerily empty street alike. Her heart was pounding with alarm and dread. She knew nothing but panic, and her feet propelled her haphazardly down the sidewalk as fast as they could, as she bawled and cried for all she was worth. She had never been so scared in her life, and she kept running, tripping, getting up, and running some more as all of her anxieties and fears boiled up and became her whole world.

Young Tina did not know how long she ran, her already peculiar childhood sense of time had been contorted in her distress, but she ran until she could no longer run. She stumbled and fell and did not get up, sobbing in great big long heaves of raw emotion that left her exhausted and drained. Her ragged breaths and whimpers caught in her throat as hiccups. Slowly, as her heart rate calmed, the sounds of the world around her reasserted themselves, the buzz of the insects, the occasional chitter of a squirrel, the songbirds calling out to each other. She knew these sounds well, being such a solitary and shy child, these sounds were her companions and friends, whenever they were not frightening her. As she sobbed on the ground, these familiar sounds did nothing to comfort her. Then, young Tina heard a faint meow. She paused her sobbing for a fraction of a second, unsure of what she had heard. When she heard only silence, she resumed her sorrowful moaning. Then, she heard it again, the anxious meow of a cat.

Sitting up, young Tina tried to ignore the aches and pains of her bruises and scratches and tried to suppress her sniffles and hiccups. There it was again, the pleading sound of a cat calling out. Wiping her eyes and her runny nose on her shirt sleeve, Tina looked around for any sign of a cat, but could see none. She did not even know where she was at first. As her tears were blinked away, Tina started to recognize landmarks, mostly bushes and hedges, and she stood up. The meow was louder this time, and she turned her head in its direction. Even then, she did not initially see it, not until it waved about. There was a paw protruding out of the mail slot of one of the houses, a house young Tina was not all that familiar with. The paw moved again, back and forth, as if it were fishing around for something, and the cat meowed again, still anxiously, still calling out for any small child, like young Tina, to pay attention to it, as it batted at the flap covering the mail slot.

Curiosity and fascination were powerful forces in a juvenile mind like Tina's and she simply forgot her own troubles as she slowly walked over to the door. The cat inside seemed to know she was approaching and doubled its efforts to attract her interaction, its meows taking on a plaintive tone that would naturally cut to the heart of most mortals. Young Tina whispered softly to the paw, reassuring it, and the cat beyond the door, that she was there. She stroked the paw softly after it stopped moving about. She was rewarded with an immediate purr as the cat flexed its pads to indicate enjoyment of the little girl's affection. The child and the animal, separated by a stout wooden door, continued this surreal exchange for a long time. As she pet the cat's extended paw, young Tina was soothed and comforted, all of her recent distress and upset draining away with each stroke on the soft fur of the appreciative feline within.

"Hi there!" Tina almost jumped into the air when the old woman spoke to her from the path leading up to the porch. She had been oblivious of anything other than the cat she was petting and had not noticed the adult's approach. A little scared once again, which was her default state when dealing with anyone, young Tina trembled, looking nervously around for somewhere to hide. The old woman just smiled and held out her hand for the little girl to shake, saying as she did, "Tina, isn't it? My, you have grown since I saw you last."

Young Tina paused in her contemplation of possible escape, looking at the adult with confusion. She did not recognize the woman, but then she rarely bothered to differentiate one adult from another, being afraid of them all equally if they were not her parents. She shrank back from the proffered hand, regarding it as a normal person would regard a poisonous snake, and she tried to hide her head in her shirt with one hand, while holding desperately onto the still protruding cat's paw, her anchor of strength against this unknown person.

Seeing Tina's reaction the owner of the house and the cat within withdrew her hand and softened her expression even more. Long a master of the art of dealing with children of all sorts and temperaments, Beverly Masterson nodded toward the cat's paw, and asked in a slightly excited tone, "Do you want to meet the rest of the cat? I'm sure she would like to meet you!" This got Tina's attention, and a minor war of instincts and apprehensions waged within her developing mind, only to lose out to curiosity and wonder. Pushing her head out of her shirt enough to look at the kindly adult, young Tina cautiously nodded her head. Beverly waited patiently for the little girl to let go of the paw and scoot out of the way, far enough to feel safe, before stepping to her door and unlocking it. The moment the key entered the lock, the paw vanished from the mail slot and the cat inside started meowing insistently for Beverly to open the door faster.

Young Tina watched, simultaneously excited and dubious, as the door opened. In a flash too fast to follow with the human eye, a large mass of fur flew out of the door and into the little girl's arms as Lady Nincompoop claimed a new playmate. The startled child had no time to object before the cat was rubbing up against her. She nudged at the little girl's hands in the demanding way cats do when they want those hands employed in the only worthwhile activity they can be other than providing food. Before she knew what was happening, young Tina found herself fully occupied with a large warm cat splayed out on her lap, petting or scratching whatever part of the creature was presented to her, which changed from moment to moment as the desires of the cat whimsically shifted.

"Would you like some milk or juice?" Tina glanced up from the demanding feline at the adult's question, her hands continuing their dutiful work. Beverly Masterson was standing there holding out a plate of cookies for the little girl on her front porch. Young Tina eagerly snatched one up, suddenly realizing how very hungry all that crying had made her, and munched on it while Lady Nincompoop complained at the lessened attention. Tina nodded yes to the old woman's question, but did not answer which. When she was presented with a cup of milk, she took it just as eagerly, drinking it down in one gulp before returning to the ever pressing task of petting the cat in her lap, who was by then demanding a full belly rub. This cat was like no other Tina had ever encountered before. Most cats were not this affectionate in her experience, usually hissing or snapping at her if she tried petting them for very long. Lady Nincompoop seemed to not know the meaning of enough.

Beverly Masterson came back out of her house once more and sat down on her swinging porch bench, humming softly as she knitted, glancing over approvingly every so often. Before long, Tina's mother arrived and showered concern on her daughter, hugging her up into her arms and fussing over all of her scrapes and bruises. Tina tried to explain what had happened to her earlier that day, but could not form the words properly, as her exhaustion finally caught up with her. Lady Nincompoop danced about below the child, batting at the air near her dangling feet and whining for her plaything to be returned to her. Tina's mom thanked Beverly for calling her and looking after her daughter until she could arrive. Beverly assured her it was no trouble at all, and remarked how, in all of her decades as a teacher, she had encountered far worse situations. Beverly assured the distraught mother that her daughter would be fine after some rest, and invited them over for tea the next evening. Lady Nincompoop protested when the little girl was carried off, but did not leave the porch, instead looking over at her mistress to make sure someone was still present to whine at.

Beverly set aside her knitting and patted her lap, the only invitation the needy cat had ever needed to leap upon it and demand further love. The teacher readily indulged her goofy cat for a few hours as the sun set, relating the ordeals of the working day to the indifferent animal. It had been a long day, and there had been many challenges, but it was over now, and as it ended, so did its troubles. After the sun had set and the moon was bright in the sky, the elderly teacher of young children retired indoors with her rambunctious pet to prepare for bed and a new day that awaited after sleep.

Dense clouds rolled in over the lane and the moon and the stars vanished in the gloom. Everything was still, the gusts of wind from the day having died away. The night was long and dark and silent, the creatures of the night did not stir. Nothing dared move or make a sound. The ominous stillness crept on hour after hour, the shadows bearing silent witness to the only living thing visible on the lane that night. Old Mrs. Habernathy had resumed her post in front of her house, her eyes never wavering from the house with the dead yard. Her glare had grown even more intense and hateful than it had been the day before, and the house with the dead yard was as silent as a tomb under her stare. Far down the lane, as far down the lane as there was lane, there came a sharp snap and an unearthly screech of sudden death, then no further sound was heard that night.

When at last the sun broke the edge of the darkness and light and heat flooded the heavens, the clouds melted away into wisps of mist, to be blown away by a sudden gust of warm wind from the east. The usual early morning chorus of birds did not sound that morning, the silence of the night lingered until those that work for their daily bread departed in their cars to their allotted occupations. Slowly, gingerly, the wild animals on the lane relaxed back into their normal activities, the unease of the previous day and night lasting longer than it ever had before. By the time Paxton Green had handed his handcrafted missives to Young Tommy that Wednesday, the lane seemed as normal as it ever was, an ever chaotic hustle and bustle of insects, animals, small children, and those adults who no longer needed to, or never had to, hold down a job.

After Young Tommy had departed with his envelopes in hand, Paxton Green checked the traps he had set up the evening before around his front yard. Finding none of them triggered, he made his way to his back yard, hoping that one of the traps there had caught his intended target. He smiled grimly when he found what he had been seeking in a trap under the old oak tree. Nodding resolutely, Paxton Green went around his yards, deactivating and gathering the remaining traps, as they were no longer needed and could potentially catch unwary animals or small children. Paxton was just pulling up the last of his traps from the front yard and setting it atop the rest in his wheelbarrow when Terrence waved to him from the sidewalk. Walking over to his low front fence, Paxton leaned against the planks for a spell as he listened to his next door neighbor complain about the horrendous noise that had woken the retiree in the middle of the night. Nodding congenially, Paxton Green agreed that such a noise was mighty disturbing, and promised to look into it, then idly wondered if perhaps it was some wild animal in distress or two such beasts engaged in a struggle of some sort that had made the ghastly sound.

By the time he went back inside his house, Terrence had been mollified of his irritation. After all, he had not honestly expected Paxton Green to have any real ready-at-hand solution to his interrupted sleep. Terrence had really only wanted to vent to someone, and Paxton Green was ever the understanding and sympathetic ear for the minor plights that occasionally disturbed the otherwise dull and monotonous routine of Terrence's retired life. If he were being honest with himself, Terrence had not really been happy living alone. Most of his life was a series of minor irritations that he had no one to share with. He knew he should look for some form of companionship, but just couldn't work up the motivation to do so. Ever since his loyal Rex had died all those years ago, he had been unable to work up the impetus for much of anything at all beyond the bare minimum needed to go on living. Complaining to his neighbors was about all he could manage these days.

As he sat in his living room, amongst the remnants of his long life, Terrence zoned out for a while, lost in nostalgia as he reminisced about his younger days, when everything made sense and there were things worth living for. This was how he spent most of his time anymore, as it was a comfortable, or at least familiar, place to be. The past never challenged him, his memories never let him down, which was more than he could say of the present and the young people in it. This day would have gone as most days went, spent in a stupor of sentimentality and remorse, had he not smelt the unmistakable odor of smoke in the air. Something was burning, and it did not smell like food. He did not know what it smelled like, other than death and decay. In an instant, Terrence was on his feet and racing to the door. It was far too hot in the season for this to be someone's fireplace, and it was against the local ordinances to burn trash or brush.

Within minutes, Terrence was stalking about his own front yard, taking a few paces in one direction and then another, sniffing the air for some clue as to the direction the smoke was coming from. It did not take him long to determine the origin of the offending odor, but it was not by smell. There was a faint haze of bluish brown smoke rising above the treetops of Paxton Green's backyard grove. Terrence hesitated. Despite his earlier complaints about the loud noise the prior night, Terrence liked Paxton and considered him an ideal neighbor. Paxton Green never worked with power tools, preferring the manual variety for every job, and refrained from the use of any tools that would make a loud noise until after noon. His house was always in good repair and the arboriculturaly obsessed old gentleman had a yard and garden that professionals would envy. Reconsidering the temptation to call the fire marshal about the illegal burn, Terrence instead chose to knock on the corner of their adjoined back fences. Surely, he thought, Paxton Green had a good reason to be burning something so noxious in his back yard.

He had to knock twice before Paxton opened his back gate and came out to talk with him. Paxton was wiping soot and ash off of his hands with a cloth as he smiled at the retiree, greeting him, "How can I help you, Terrence?"

"I smelled smoke. Are you burning something?"

"Yep."

"Garbage?"

"Yes and no."

Terrence frowned slightly, "You know that's not allowed by the city, right?"

Paxton's smile never slipped or faltered, "Yep."

Terrence wrinkled his brow, not sure how to argue with that, "Well, ok then." Paxton just nodded, still smiling. Terrence sniffed dramatically before remarking, "Smells awful bad."

Paxton nodded, "Yep. Was awful bad."

Looking around as if he expected to see something else to say, Terrence asked, "So... about how much longer you think that smell will last?"

"Oh, I don't reckon it'll be much longer. Mostly ash by now."

Terrence gave up and nodded. He was unlikely to get any more out of his favorite neighbor on the matter, not without being rude about it. As he watched Paxton return to his back yard with a shovel, Terrence almost went back inside, but reconsidered, not sure how long the smell would actually linger. Remembering that it had been several days since he had left his house for any reason, Terrence sighed and set out for the nearby park. He could use a walk, and not just for the fresh air. It took him longer than it would have others to walk down the lane, not from any disability or obstacle. He simply had no reason to be in any hurry. Life may have gotten disturbingly fast around him or he may have just slowed down, either way he was in no rush. He had nowhere in particular to be anyway.

It was not only because he had no urgency in his meander, but also because it had been so long since he had been to the park, that it took so long to realize that he was walking further into the lane, toward the end of the cul-de-sac, not out toward the park. Terrence only noticed his stray course as he stood looking at the house with the dead yard. For awhile he did not move. He just stood there on the sidewalk in front of the house with the dead yard, staring at the looming structure, no bigger than any of the houses around it, yet capturing his attention like no other. There was an allure to the decaying building, an attraction in its deterioration. The weather-worn, paintless boards that seemed only seconds away from dropping off the walls of the vacant structure did not move, yet they seemed to pulse. No, pulse was the wrong word. Pulse implied life, and there was no life to the house with the dead yard. No, they seemed to shiver, but without motion. Terrence heard no sound, felt no draw, but still he felt captivated by the ominous and inexorable presence that seemed to emanate without any visible means from the house with the dead yard.

Icy cold fingers closed painfully on his shoulder, and Terrence squawked and broke his entranced gaze to stare at the haggard but fierce face of Old Mrs. Habernathy, her piercing eyes filled with hate and rage. Her eyes were not directed at Terrence, but her words were as she firmly stated, "There is nothing to see here. Move along."

Terrence shrank away from the older woman when she released her grip, shuddering as the blood rushed back into his shoulder. Without looking back toward the house with the dead yard, Terrence stumbled away, this time in the correct direction toward the park. He stole glances back at Old Mrs. Habernathy every so often, in disbelief of the whole encounter. It was while he was looking backward but walking forward down the sidewalk that he almost collided into Young Tommy, who was distracted as well, confirming the address on a letter. Luckily for both of the men, Young Tommy looked up at the right moment and managed to dance out of the way of the retiree. Terrence mumbled an apology and hurried off toward the park.

Young Tommy thought nothing of the near accident, a matter of routine in his line of work, and turned into Liola's drive to deliver her daily correspondence. Passing the pink pelican statues, he reached the door and then stopped with a frown. Something was wrong. Liola never let him actually reach the door without calling out for him to enter, not once in the entire time he had been delivering mail on the lane. With some fear for her wellbeing, Young Tommy knocked on Liola's door. There was no response. Now he was really concerned. Knocking again, only louder, Young Tommy broke out in a minor sweat when silence continued to be the response. What he did next was against every rule in the book as well as several laws, but he did not hesitate for a second. This was no ordinary house, and Liola was no typical customer. Young Tommy opened the door and entered the house.

Once inside, Young Tommy called out her name, but still received no reply. Entering the 'room', he found her customary chair empty, and unlike the day before there was no sign of mishap to be seen. The chair looked forlorn and incomplete without its owner, seemingly without purpose yet still present, unable to be anything other than what it was, but useless all the same. Young Tommy went from room to room in the house, calling out for Liola, but finding no sign that she was there that morning. It was while he was in one of the empty and unused upstairs rooms that he heard it, a low muted humming sound, similar to a song, but just the one verse over and over again. He had never heard the song before, at least he did not think he had, but that was the least of his thoughts upon hearing the song. Instead, he tried to determine its origin, but could barely discern it at all, as if it were coming from some place far away, or long ago. It was a haunting sound, made all the more eerie for its short repetition and low tone.

As he wandered about, attempting to find where the sound was loudest, he happened to glance out the window into the back yard, and gave a cry of shock and anguish. There, in the middle of the back yard, was Liola, digging as if she were gardening. Only, Liola did not garden, nor was she digging with a trowel or other instruments suited to the task. Liola was digging in the dirt with her hands, as she lay on her side, her useless legs trailing after her. She was covered in dirt, from her disarrayed hair to her unshod feet. Even her nightgown, torn in several places, was filthy from the soil. As she dug, aimlessly and without any apparent urgency, she kept humming the same short nameless tune with a mindless grin plastered on her glazed face. Young Tommy ran to the phone. Wilber arrived huffing and puffing within minutes, Candice arrived a few minutes later carrying her doctor's bag. It took a whole hour for the ambulance to show up, and another hour passed before it left. A taxi followed the ambulance, shared by Wilber and Candice in troubled silence. Young Tommy stayed behind to lock up Liola's house before returning to his rounds. The mail still needed to be delivered, and though he was running late and his nerves were shot and his smile would not return that day, Tommy would deliver the mail.

He stopped at Ella and Ida's to sit and rest for a minute, trying to collect his wits, willing his hands to stop shaking, as he related the incident to a concerned Ella. Noticing that Ida was not present, he asked where she was.

Ella frowned, remembering her own harrowing ordeal from the night before, "She is upstairs resting. She twisted her ankle yesterday. We thought it was a break at first, but luck was on our side."

Young Tommy expressed his condolences and concern, and listened attentively as Ella related the whole incident to him. Feeling a lot calmer, though still very distressed, Tommy returned to work, wishing Ella the best of luck with Ida's recovery. Ella waved goodbye to the departing postman, then frowned as she looked across the road again at the ever present neighborhood blight, the house with the dead yard. Trembling with unease, Ella once more abandoned the tray of coconut macaroons on the porch table under the protective silk cloth and retreated inside, away from the offending sight. Only when the door was safely shut, did she feel safe once more, and her breathing subconsciously relaxed. Ida was still asleep upstairs, so Ella bustled into their kitchen to check on the tray of blueberry scones, which were coming along nicely, before pulling out a stick of butter from the fridge to warm and soften in a small clay dish on top of the warm oven.

While waiting for the delicious pastries to finish baking, Ella began the preparations for dinner, washing and slicing a dozen fresh potatoes and shredding a small mountain of cheese she would later combine with diced onions and leeks into a casserole. The oven timer dinged behind her at the same time there came a timid knock on the front door, so she did not at first realize she had a guest. The knock came again as she was setting the hot tray onto the stovetop to cool, so she hurried over to see who had come calling. She opened the door to the grinning face of the youngest Murphy boy, and the jumbled handful of assorted wild, and pilfered, flowers he was presenting to her as a bouquet. Several of the flowers were wilted and others had broken stems or missing petals, but Ella thanked the charming young child for the thoughtful and pretty gift.

He grinned even wider as he said, "Oh, they're not for you!" Ella's smile faltered for a second before he added, "They're for Ida! Bobby's mom said she was sick, so I brought her flowers to make her better!"

Ella's smile returned in full force as she laughed at the boy's kindness. She thanked him again, this time for thinking of Ida in her 'time of need'. She invited the youngest Murphy boy inside for a freshly baked blueberry scone and butter, an invitation he would have been mad to turn down, and they sat in the kitchen as he ate and related his latest impish adventures. She tried to get him to eat or talk, but not both at the same time, yet smiled when he forgot her admonitions minutes later. After he had helped himself to not one but three scones layered in melted butter, not to mention the pair of macaroons he had scarfed down earlier on her porch before knocking, the youngest Murphy boy excused himself.

He paused at the door, looking up at Ella with that irresistible grin of his, asking "Can I have two more scones? For some friends!" Ella tutted at the child's transparent greed, but as the young boy left her house at a run, he had two scones in his jacket pockets, wrapped in paper napkins. The youngest Murphy boy made a bee-line for Bobby's house, wanting to deliver the scones, and the macaroons he had also pocketed, to the twins while they were still fresh. As usual, his entrance into Bobby's house was loud and unannounced as he raced by Bobby's mother, ignoring her calls for caution and restraint. Taking the stairs two at a time, he burst into the twin's room a little more quietly than he had the house, but he always was a little more careful and controlled around the twins. As he regaled them with his exploits and fed them the double bounty of the day, the youngest Murphy boy basked in the undivided attention the twins always paid him. His and Bobby's near catastrophic collision with Leo Tuttle took shape as an epic adventure where they were nearly bested by a strange and powerful wizard, only to emerge victorious by mere happenstance. The subsequent punishments the two boys had earned were transformed into just penitence for unintentionally broken oaths of loyalty and honor. He was about to launch into a grand retelling of his singular conquest of the secret backyard jungle when the twins' mother entered the room to herd the excited boy out before he outstayed his welcome.

Bobby met the youngest Murphy boy in the hallway, and together the pair raced down the stairs three at a time in unintended defiance of the house rules before bursting outside in an explosion of laughter and energy. Without speaking a word toward that end, the pair of boys fell into a race with each other as they ran toward the house with the pink pelican statues, each determined to arrive first and so attain the transient accolade of fastest. More often than not, the boys would reach the hedge with the hidden hole simultaneously and squabble good naturedly over who had won for far longer than the actual race had taken. Today, however, their race was cut short very abruptly by the commanding voice of Beverly Masterson. They were surprised as much by her sharp command to stop as by her presence on the lane this early in the day. Beverly was never home at this hour, not on a weekday when school was in session, so when she called out to them to stop and come to her, Bobby and the youngest Murphy boy obeyed more out of curiosity than any imperative to mind an authoritative adult.

Their curiosity did not impel them to hurry, however, and they took as long as they thought they could get away with to walk back to her drive and up to her house. For her part, Beverly did not appear to notice, as she had ducked back inside to fetch two small boxes, each wrapped securely in plain brown paper and red twine. She handed a box to each boy, and instructed them to deliver them to two separate houses. Even though they had long ago paid their debt to the elderly teacher, the boys would still do any reasonable task she asked of them without question. Like most adults, Beverly Masterson thought of the pair as the mischievous little scamps they were, but was one of the few adults on the lane who treated them as if they could be trusted. She had always believed, as a teacher, that if you treat children as deserving of respect, they aspire to be worthy, and in all of her dealings with Bobby and the youngest Murphy boy, she had given them respect and earned theirs.

After briefly paying their respects to Lady Nincompoop, the boys ran off in separate directions with Beverly's gifts. Bobby would deliver the one marked for Ida while the youngest Murphy boy saw to it that young Tina's mother got the other. Despite their well earned reputation, Beverly gave no more thought to the safety of her packages in the hands of the two youths, instead turning to Lady Nincompoop, who was frantically trying to unravel a loose thread hanging from her red sweater. Chastising the silly animal for its kittenish behavior, especially ridiculous for a cat as old as Lady Nincompoop was, Beverly snatched the thread from reach and went inside to fetch a pair of scissors.

The youngest Murphy boy dashed down the street, weaving on and off the sidewalk and around the various parked cars with the practiced incaution of a suburbanite child. He held the box, carefully wrapped in brown paper, under one arm as he used the other for balance and occasionally to deflect his forward motion off of any object he did not see far enough in advance. He greeted the car that stopped short in front of him and blared its horn angrily with a fit of laughter and a half-hearted wave, not stopping to face the consequences of his near-collision.

The youngest Murphy boy took a shortcut across Mrs. Tilly's yard, but was uncharacteristically careful where he placed his feet so as to not damage anything. He liked Mrs. Tilly and he really liked her garden, and how it was always changing. It felt like a magical realm of plants and flowers and faerie folk, one that would shift about when you were not looking so as to hide its ever ethereal secrets from the outside world. There were a few established shrubs and trees that never changed with the rest, and these the youngest Murphy boy imagined were the true gateways into another world, a world of myth and adventure and beauty that would put even Mrs. Tilly's horticultural efforts to shame. This was a world he had never seen except in daydreams, but was a world he was convinced was as real as anything else had ever been.

Right now, though, the youngest Murphy boy had no time for wild fantasies of lands beyond the mortal ken, and he paid no more mind to Mrs. Tilly's latest additions and alterations to her front yard than was necessary to navigate across it without leaving a trace. Right now, he was on a mission, and a mission to a small child like the youngest Murphy boy was the most important thing that has ever been or ever will be in the world. As soon as he set foot on the sidewalk beyond the lawn, the youngest Murphy boy was off like a shot once more with all possible speed toward his destination, a house he had never personally been to but vaguely knew the location of. He would deliver the package entrusted to his care dutifully, assuming he did not get distracted along the way.

Luckily for the care package Beverly Masterson had put together for the little girl who had injured herself outside of her house, the youngest Murphy boy successfully reached the house near the end of the lane without incident or diversion, clattering noisily up the porch steps and banging unnecessarily loudly on the front door. Young Tina's mother opened the door to the youngest Murphy boy, who looked up and announced with a grin that he was delivering the box entrusted to him. Taking the package from the young boy, she smiled and thanked him for his service. Nodding enthusiastically in acknowledgement, the youngest Murphy boy blinked as a small girl about his age peeked out from behind the legs of her mother, only to squeak and hide again. Cocking his head quizzically to one side, the youngest Murphy boy chirped a cheerful greeting to the other child.

When no answer came, other than the little girl's hands tightening visibly in their death grip on her mother's pants, the youngest Murphy boy looked up at the adult with confusion and concern, asking, "Is she okay?"

Tina's mother smiled at the friendly boy on her porch, "Oh, she's just shy."

"Did I scare her? I'm sorry!"

"Oh, no. It's okay. She's afraid of everything, aren't you Tina?" Tina's only answer was another, softer, squeak, muffled by the back of her mother's legs. Her mother turned back to the youngest Murphy boy, continuing, "Don't worry, she'll grow out of it."

A little curious and concerned, having never encountered another child this bashful in the past, the youngest Murphy boy tried once more to talk to the little girl hiding behind her parent, "Hey, are you okay?" No answer came, as before, but he persisted, "Do you want to come play with me and Bobby? We could go on an adventure!"

Only silence responded from the secreted figure, and after Tina's mother thanked him for trying, the youngest Murphy boy shrugged his shoulders, waved goodbye, and dashed off, eager to rendezvous with Bobby to tell him all about the strange little girl who said nothing that he had not really met. He was already imagining an elaborate story that would explain her strange condition and hatching a grand scheme they could attempt that would magically cure her of the malady. Most of these mad notions would be forgotten entirely before he met up with Bobby, and none of them would be acted upon, but the boys would delight in play-acting out the more fantastical of the scenarios in the coming weeks.

Preoccupied as he was in his daydreams, the youngest Murphy boy only avoided colliding with Travis at high velocity by an outstretched hand. Travis caught the child by the chest, slowing him down in time for the boy to notice the adult and take off on a new, obstacle free, vector. The door-to-door salesman did not even get a chance to reprimand the child for running around so haphazardly as the boy disappeared behind a hedge. Grunting his annoyance to no one in particular, Travis picked up his sample case from where he had dropped it and dusted it off before continuing his interrupted circuit around the lane. Methodically, with the precision of a clock and the determination of one who cannot be deterred by kind or unkind words, Travis stopped at every house on the lane, one after the other, to disturb the days of the residents, soliciting a product none of them needed and few cared to learn about.

The product he was attempting to market was not harmful, was not defective, was not cheaply made, and was not a scam. However, the product was not at all useful or necessary in anyone's lives. Still, he diligently made his rounds from one unimpressed homeowner to the next, extolling the virtues of his device and imploring them to consider the possibilities, trying to convince them they needed something they did not. One by one, doors were closed in his face, and Travis would nod, say thank you, and move on to the next house. He had not made a sale in days, yet he never succumbed to the temptations of his aggravation to express irritation to anyone he met. While he did not see his profession as irksome or intrusive, he nevertheless understood he was an interloper in these peoples' lives, an uninvited outsider imposing upon their time in order to sell something. He understood their reactions even as he resented them.

Another door shut in his face and another opportunity to make a sale that day vanished behind varnished wood. Travis sighed once more and walked back to the sidewalk. He had to make a sale today, he was far behind quota and running low on money. It had been a hard quarter for him, at the end of a difficult year, and it was all he could do to keep his despondency and desperation from showing to his potential customers. If Travis had not needed so much to make a sale, it was unlikely he would have turned onto the path leading up to the house with the dead yard. The eerie, haunting appearance of the house with the dead yard, the deathly silence and stillness that hung about the place, invisible yet still noticeable, seeped slowly through his determination, and a growing sense of unease and danger crept over him. Every step felt like an irreversible movement toward inevitability, every inch closer to the door flooded Travis with impending panic, yet he could not stop. He could not look away from the yawning chasm that was opening before him, welcoming him to enter the house with the dead yard, beckoning him into the darkness beyond the door, enticing him into an oblivion with an unspoken promise of no more cares and no more worries. All he had to do was step forward, one more step and he...

He reeled back from the sharp pain in his right ear, as if someone had jabbed a hot needle into his brain, stumbling away from the door and off the porch, barely catching himself before he fell down on the path. Looking around in agony, Travis found no attacker, seeing no one about except for one particularly fearsome looking old woman who was glaring murderously past him at the house, but she was standing far away, across the dead yard, on the sidewalk near the house. Pulling his hand away, Travis looked at it as if expecting blood or some other sign of injury, but found none. The pain faded as immediately as it had come, leaving a befuddled door-to-door solicitor looking about in confusion. Gradually, recovering his wits and concluding that the jarring pain had been entirely in his head, Travis looked back again at the old woman, suddenly very self conscious and disturbed by her presence. As unflappable as he thought he was, Travis realized he wanted to be anywhere but there. With great urgency, he walked as quickly as he could with any hint of dignity up the path and down the sidewalk, away from the house with the dead yard, away from the angry old woman, and away from the lane forever.

He did not look back, he did not look from side to side, he only looked ahead, toward anywhere but the lane. It was while he was so intently focused on not looking both ways that he crossed in front of a taxi, which was fortunately being driven cautiously by a very alert Marshall. Marshall had experienced many close calls on this particular lane and was driving slowly while keeping a diligent eye out for stray animals and humans alike, juvenile or otherwise. He was not in the habit of needing to repeat lessons, so stopped well short of the anxious and perplexed man who walked right out in front of his taxi. Eyeing the stranger with incredulity until he had passed, Marshall continued driving with great care down the lane. He came to a stop in front of one of his more frequent customers, the ever perplexing Leo Tuttle.

The odd little man was waiting for his arrival and climbed into the back of the cab without a word. It took a great deal of time, as a large heavy box preceded him into the taxi, occupying most of the back bench of the vehicle and drawing Marshall's interest. When the box growled, Marshall turned around to stare at it and the small man sitting beside it.

A little upset, Marshall demanded information, "What the hell is that?"

Leo remained deadpan and entirely without humor as he answered, "It's a box."

"No, I mean what's in the box?"

"What I put in there."

Marshall would have ejected anyone else at that answer, but since Leo had been providing him business reliably for so many years, the taxi driver held his temper in check and looked directly into Leo's eyes with an expression that brooked no nonsense, "What did you put in the box, Leo? What the hell did you just put in my car?"

Leo sighed, and realized that some manner of real communication would be necessary before the journey would commence. Knowing he would face similar, or even more intense, questioning if he tried to take the bus with his package, Leo attempted to diffuse the situation at hand, "I am returning a very exotic pet to the store of its origin. You needn't worry. Inside the box it is entirely harmless, and I promise it will remain in the box until after I reach my destination."

"Yeah? Why are you returning it?"

"It... recently inflicted grave harm to my person. I no longer wish to abide its presence in my home."

"It injured you? But you just said it was harmless."

"It is harmless. In the box. When it harmed me, it was not in the box."

Marshall was not satisfied with this answer. He was not at all enthusiastic with the idea of transporting exotic, and apparently dangerous, wildlife in his taxi, especially not when all that stood between him and it appeared to be constructed of nothing more than standard cardboard. The din it launched into inside the box was doing nothing to ease his concerns. He had previously seen the extent of Leo's injuries when he had driven the man home from the hospital, and doubted thick corrugated paper would act as an adequate barrier against whatever had caused them. He had to make a decision though, and disregarding his better judgment, he chose to allow the box and its recalcitrant owner to remain in his cab, at least until he got them to the address Leo requested. Grunting in extreme annoyance, Marshall turned around again, to devote his entire attention to his driving, both out of caution for errant lifeforms and to distract his attention away from the large angry box behind him. As they passed by the bus that was unloading passengers at its stop on the lane, Marshall wished his reticent passenger had chosen that conveyance instead for his errand.

One of the passengers that stepped off the bus with a heavy sigh, exhausted by the events of the day so far, was Wilber Tumbleburry. Wilber momentarily forgot his own troubles to watch the taxi with idle interest as it proceeded down the lane, trying to discern the nature of the loud sounds emanating from within the cab. In response to a mild grunt, Wilber glanced back at the bus and backed out of the way of the other disembarking passenger, an equally troubled and exhausted Candice. The two had decided the bus was the more suitable option for their return trip, there being no urgency in their return. They had initially intended to discuss the matter that found them at the hospital during the bus ride, but silence had been their discourse for the whole ride. Both preferred their own counsel to that of the other, turning and churning their thoughts and theories in their minds. No useful conclusions or epiphanies resulted, no measure of comfort was achieved, but at least they had not argued.

Having arrived, they no longer had to continue in each others' company, nor did they desire to do so. Without a word shared between them since they had left the hospital, Candice and Wilber Tumbleburry parted ways. Candice headed straight home. Wilber wandered toward the nearby park, simply so he could avoid walking in the same direction, next to Liola's other nearest friend in the world. Candice walked slowly, still in shock from seeing her dearest friend in such a condition earlier that day. She walked slowly, thinking of the unfolding events that she herself played such a prominent part in so recently. She walked slowly as she tried to process all of the emotions and feelings that had jumbled up in the back of her mind as the most stable aspects of her life unraveled all about her, in front of her, in her own hands, behind glass walls, and in hallways waiting anxiously for news of any kind. Candice walked slowly because she knew that at any moment she would break down and her world would fall apart and rain down upon her path in a torrent of tears and anguish.

Despite a lifetime of medical experience, Candice did not understand what had happened. She understood the terms, she understood the science behind the terms, and she understood how those terms related to what her friend had suffered, but she still did not understand how such a thing had occurred to Liola. How could it have happened so fast? How was it not detected long before it occurred? Why were there none of the known warning signs? None of it made sense, even as it all fit so neatly together. Candice was now reeling from the consequences, predictably blaming herself for not having the foresight, for not being observant enough, for having missed what must have been obvious for so long, for not saving her one true friend in life from one of the worst fates imaginable. Candice stumbled safely home somehow and collapsed on her bed, drained both physically and emotionally. Yet sleep refused to come. Her brain refused to let her rest, preferring to torture her with suppositions of choices not made and illusions of possible warning signs she must have missed or ignored. She allowed her brain to analyze every last one. She allowed her mind to torment her and haunt her with a building guilt that she felt was just. Liola, dear sweet loyal Liola, was in a coma, and it had to be Candice's fault somehow. No other conclusion could make sense of the unfairness of it all.

After sobbing for an hour, the inevitabilities of biological life persisted and reminded her that she was not herself in a coma. Candice got up and continued to live, though she diligently managed to be thoroughly miserable while doing so. Eventually, even as she chastised herself relentlessly, she began to contemplate more practical and pragmatic matters, such as what to do next, how to move on, what life would be like now that Liola had been effectively removed. Though she knew full well these were all subjects needing further thought, she still did not want to contemplate them at the moment, and tried to think of something else, anything else, but her own future. One matter that eventually wandered to the forefront of her muddled thoughts was what would become of Liola's house and things. Liola had long ago designated Candice as her proxy for all medical decisions in case of incapacitation, but Candice had never asked who held Liola's power of attorney, or for that matter, who was her executor. Candice suspected, with some disgust, that Wilber Tumbleburry had been entrusted with those duties, and realized that she would have to deal closely with the didactic little man in the future if that were indeed the case.

Thinking of the 'professor' brought a new flood of guilt to mind. Wilber probably blamed her as much as she blamed herself for what had happened. That she thought he would be right in such blame only enhanced her antipathy toward the man. Then, the most revolting presupposition occurred to her, and she felt sudden nausea at the possibility. Suppose Wilber did not blame her? It would be just like the loathsome prig to dismiss her culpability out of hand, despite their mutual animosity. How dare he. Candice was not at all sure she could live with the guilt she was inflicting upon herself, but she knew she absolutely would not be able to suffer through Wilber Tumbleburry's absolution. She spent a full minute vocally cursing and swearing at the open air, calling down future curses upon the 'professor' if he dared forgive her so easily.

There was a knock at her door, and Candice startled. She was not expecting company, and felt entirely unsuited to entertain. In her mind, there was only one person who could possibly be calling upon her at this hour of the day, and he was the last person she wanted to ever see, much less right now. Snarling up her face in preparation to spit venom and invective at Wilber Tumbleburry, Candice opened the door in a fury, and then melted into a ball of tears in the arms of Young Tommy. The pair were not the closest of friends, but there was no animosity between them, just as there was no animosity between Young Tommy and Wilber Tumbleburry. The friendly postman had always been an unacknowledged intermediary between the pair, taken for granted all these years in the towering shadow of Liola. Now, he was the closest friend she had left, and together they mourned their mutual tragedy.

After awhile, the two had cried themselves out, for the moment at least. They sat down in Candice's living room for some tea and silence. They occasionally attempted to break the somber mood with inane chitchat or fond memories of their mutual friend, but mostly with inane chitchat, the more inane the better. Neither really wanted to trigger another round of anguish and weeping. So the afternoon was spent, and gradually, as Young Tommy succeeded in distracting her from her own pernicious self-incriminations, Candice grew tired and dozed off where she sat, slipping into a sweet, simple sleep, where there were no dreams and no nightmares to haunt her. Young Tommy got up quietly, covered her in a blanket to keep the chill at bay, and slipped out of the house. Hoping the worst was past, both for himself and for her, the postman strolled down the lane, sniffing occasionally as his feelings of loss suddenly welled up. He marveled at all of the subtle little signs of life all around him, the motion of the wind in the leaves of the trees, the ballet of the birds in the sky as they swirled and swooped to and fro in their endless hunt for sustenance, at the timelessness of nature, even in this highly artificed environment. His grief was not pacified, but it was soothed, at least for a while. He was resolved not to let his anguish overcome him. Somehow, he knew that Liola would not want her friends falling apart over her condition.

"Are you okay?" Tommy blinked away the tears that were blurring his view of the clouds, and looked with a partial smile at Amanda and her father standing in front of him on the sidewalk. Their concern was visible, and he nodded to assure them he was alright. Amanda prodded, "What's wrong?"

"Oh... I'll be okay. It's my friend. She's... she's very ill, and I'm worried for her." Tommy suddenly found himself enveloped in an unsolicited hug by the very pregnant young woman, a hug that he appreciated and reciprocated in the spirit of empathy it was intended. He did not really want to go into the details of why he was crying, and thankfully neither Amanda nor George requested them. Neither needed to know the specifics to feel sympathy for another human in need. Both father and daughter had encountered enough troubles in their own lives to identify and appreciate the emotional pain of others. While Amanda communicated her rapport through her embrace, George placed a firm hand on Tommy's shoulder and smiled with a compassion that only a lifetime of experience can summon. Amanda had never known Liola, and George had only heard of her from others on the lane, and neither knew she was the one being mourned. It did not matter. Their neighbor needed them, and so they were there for him.

When they finally parted ways, and Tommy headed toward his house to await the night sky and his beloved stars, he was still tearing up, but was glowing a little from the warmth and affection he had not expected. George and Amanda continued toward Ella and Ida's house for afternoon tea and scones. George was silently but visibly proud of his daughter's selfless act of kindness. For her part, Amanda had changed the topic, returning to their prior discussion of what sorts of flowers to paint on the nursery walls for her baby, letting thoughts of new life naturally overtake their concerns for those already alive. They had been making a list, a very extensive catalogue, of all of the delightfully exotic and stunning flora on display both among the gardens and lawns of the lane as well as in the nearby park. Amanda pointed out each variety that caught her fancy and George dutifully recorded the species in a little note pad he kept in his pocket for such extemporaneous observations. When his daughter had remarked on the astounding diversity of flowers growing in the wild of the park, outside of the deliberate arrangements of the diligent gardeners of the lane, George had hypothesized that most of the flowers had to be introduced, as they were not native breeds. He supposed they had spread beyond their controlled environs on the lane, thriving unhindered in the park beyond the designs of their original cultivators, long after the fashions that had inspired their original introductions had passed.

Amanda was quizzing him on each of the unique strains she had noted in the park as they knocked on Ella and Ida's door and waited to be let in, testing his theory against his memory of when he had seen such a flower on the lane in the years prior. George was spared from this operose enterprise by the door swinging open and a very tired looking Ella welcoming them to her home with hugs and imprints of baking flour from her apron and mittens. Their conversation instantly and naturally shifted to Ida's health and wellbeing, and further thoughts on flora migrations were postponed to another day and another walk in the park. They had just settled down into comfortable chairs around the kitchen table with warm scones and warm butter set before them when they were joined by Ida, limping and refusing any assistance as she took a seat herself. It was a little embarrassing for their guests to watch as Ella persistently fussed over Ida and Ida kept insisting she did not need to be coddled to such infantile levels.

When, at last Ida was able to assert her capability to tend to herself and convince Ella to sit down and stop pestering her, the mood lightened once again and the conversation turned to the inescapable topic of the imminent nativity. Most men in such a circumstance would have been uncomfortable, but George was even more enthusiastic about the expected arrival of his grandchild than his daughter was. This was a truly remarkable feat, considering that Amanda's excitement was all that it should be for a woman with child. Many scones were consumed as were several pots of tea as every aspect of what to expect when you are expecting and what preparations were possible and advisable was brought up in turn and discussed at length. Ella waxed poetic about Ida's own granddaughter, born only the year before, and all of the troubles her son had encountered as a newly minted father. From childbirth to child rearing, the advice seemed never-ending, and would have been except for an unnecessarily loud banging on their front door. Such heraldings were well known to all residents of the lane as announcing the presence of a child. Ella, tutting to herself that they still had much to learn about being civilized, opened the door to Bobby and the youngest Murphy boy.

Grinning up at her in an attempt to be endearingly innocent, they rightly appeared like a pair of devilish little imps, fresh from some naughty little exploit, guilty of something yet fully knowing there was no proof of their misdeeds other than their own demeanor. Ella pouted and then smiled knowingly. These young boys were nothing but trouble, yet there was not an adult on the lane they could not charm, and Ella was among the easiest to sway. Their smirks slipped slightly when Ida limped up behind her partner to frown down upon them, but only for a moment. Ida was a tougher target, but they had won her over in the past, and they had no illusions that she would withstand their charisma, even with her injury souring her mood. Showing their teeth as they smiled even wider than before, the youngest Murphy boy asked the pair if Bobby could have one of the scones he had tried earlier in the day, and when the couple agreed to his request, he asked if he too could have another scone. Their admonishments about his greed did nothing to dissuade their cheerful expressions and insistent pleading looks, and after a pathetically short period, the elder pair relented and invited the boys in to enjoy the pastries.

The boys were introduced to Amanda, who they had never met before, by George, who they knew well. They momentarily forgot about the scones they were there for when they caught sight of Amanda's swollen belly. Being young children, and not at all suitably versed in proper manners and decorum, they immediately commented on her condition in the most ostentatious and noisy manner imaginable. The adults took turns scolding and correcting their misconception, and then had to explain what pregnancy was to the pair, at least as much as was necessary for them to grasp that a child was growing inside of her, and would soon emerge into the world as a baby. This explanation did not quench their curiosity. Instead it caused them to become even more intrigued with Amanda and her bulge, reaching out to touch it, only stopping at the last possible moment to ask if it was okay to do so. When Amanda nodded with a warm smile, first the youngest Murphy boy then Bobby held their hands against the curve of her belly. Bobby said it felt just like a basketball, but before anyone could correct him, the youngest Murphy boy yelped and yanked his hand back suddenly.

Looking simultaneously guilty and offended, the youngest Murphy boy looked around at the assembled adults before saying, "It kicked me!"

The room burst into merry laughter and the young boy felt slightly embarrassed for his naiveté. Amanda took his small hand and placed it back on her belly as they all assured him that was perfectly natural for a baby to do every so often. Bobby asked if it was going to kick him too and moved his hands about to find the ideal spot to feel the baby's movement inside of its mother. Chuckling, Ella took the two boys by their arms and guided them away from the expectant mother to some empty chairs and the hot buttered scones set out on the table in front of them. She instructed them to eat while their food was still warm. Once their eyes latched onto the delicious pastries and their brains registered the smells once more, the boys forgot about the baby and launched into their snacks with their typical enthusiasm.

While the boys ate, the adults returned to their previous conversation about all of the details a new mother would need to consider before and immediately after a birth. The children tuned them out completely. They quickly scarfed down the scones they had been served and were well into a third one each by the time Ella glanced their way again. She was not a parsimonious person, but was mindful of potentially spoiling the boys. She did not want them to develop the idea that they could always pig out at her and Ida's expense. The moment Bobby and the youngest Murphy boy were finished with their current serving, she was behind them, snatching up their dirty dishes and insisting they wash their hands and faces. Their hands were barely dry before they found themselves out the door and being told to go play. They would have eaten more had they gotten the chance, but the youngest Murphy boy and Bobby were equally eager to return to their adventures of the day, and they ran off giggling without any thought given to the welcome they had worn out. Being this close to the end of the lane, the pair naturally headed toward Candice's back yard, and the jungle yard beyond it, having already forgotten the recent ban on playing there.

The boys rounded the corner of Candice's house to her back yard and skidded to a panicked stop. Candice was in her back yard. This came as quite a surprise to both boys, as Candice was never in her back yard, at least, they had never encountered her there. Ducking back around the corner to gain cover from the house, Bobby and the youngest Murphy boy peeked around to see if she had noticed them. Candice did not seem to be noticing anything at the moment. She was sitting on one of her ordinarily unused deck benches, wrapped in a blanket despite the heat, staring out at nothing and everything simultaneously. She had a thousand yard gaze that the boys had seen before, a gaze that adults wore when they were very deep in thought or very sad and forlorn. Candice did not appear to be very deep in thought, and was not moving much except to breathe.

Bobby tugged on the youngest Murphy boy's sleeve, in a silent signal that they should leave, not wanting to disturb the adult and feeling they should make good their escape before they were discovered trespassing on her property. Bobby instinctively knew they were intruding where they were not wanted. For the first time in their many games throughout the years, he realized they should not be there, that there was a reason beyond the rules of adults they so frequently ignored that they would be unwelcome here. The youngest Murphy boy did not budge, continuing to stare at the distraught woman as she shivered and sighed. Bobby got more insistent with his tugging, but the youngest Murphy boy simply pushed him away in annoyance. He had never seen an adult this sad before. He had never seen anyone this sad before. Reaching up, he extracted Bobby's hand from his shirt and walked out into the back yard. Candice did not appear to notice, and Bobby whispered, far too loudly, at him to stop. The youngest Murphy boy walked slowly toward Candice, expecting at any moment that she would react, that she would look up at him with a scowl and a sharp reprimand, and he would be in the most trouble he had ever been in his short life. Candice did not move, her eyes still unfocused and her mind still a million miles away. Bobby gave up trying to call his friend back and watched with the universal childhood fear of getting caught being naughty. The youngest Murphy boy continued walking slowly toward Candice, step by step, until he was standing right in front of her, still unnoticed.

The youngest Murphy boy reached inside one of his pockets and pulled out a soiled paper napkin, unwrapping it and extending it toward the impassive adult. Crumbs rolled off the edges of the napkin as the youngest Murphy boy asked Candice, "Are you hungry?"

Candice's eyes focused then, and she found herself staring at a small little boy standing in her back yard, holding out a blueberry scone, crushed and crumbling and soaked in butter. She looked at the scone, then at the boy, then back at the scone as her brain attempted to bridge the gap from the abyss of grief it had only moments before been mired in to the scene before her. She tried to process the incongruity and seeming randomness of what was happening. The small boy, whose name escaped her, looked worried, and she realized he was worried about her. He was worried, and he was trying to offer her comfort in the form of a questionable baked good. Her despondency broke in the face of this unsolicited and unexpected gesture of kindness and concern from one far too young to understand what she was going through. She smiled and blinked away fresh tears as she nodded her head and reached out slowly to accept the gift. Uninvited, the small boy sat down on the bench next to her, and patted her arm in mimicry of how he had likely observed adults comforting each other as she took a cautious bite out of the soggy scone.

It was still warm and it was delicious, and it was the best thing Candice could remember consuming recently. The scone became the sole focus of her attention for awhile as she tried to remember the last time she had eaten a meal, and before she knew it, the pastry was gone and she was licking the butter from her fingers. Looking down at the boy, she smiled and hugged him, saying, "Thank you. That was just what I needed." There was a soft crunch of dirt and Candice looked up to see another boy, whom she recognized as Bobby, walking toward them nervously. She smiled at him too and waved him over. Bobby took a seat on the bench on her other side, and she hugged them both while trying to ignore their patronizing platitudes that it would all be okay. She knew it would not all be okay, but that was okay. Life was far too complex for such simplicities, and her life would never be the same, but that too was okay. Candice knew she had a lot more mourning to do before she could even begin to consider what the rest of her life would be like, but life would go on and she would eventually be okay.

When she had hugged enough, or at least enough for the moment, she thanked the boys and assured them she was better now. They grinned and ran off to have carefree adventures full of mirth and merriment absent of any real tragedy or danger. She smiled wistfully at the innocence and sincerity of youth. Candice thought back to her own childhood, so distant now, and how little complication there was then, how the simplest of things seemed to mean so much yet mattered so little. She did not miss her childhood, not like so many did, but she still treasured her memories of that time in her life. Candice took a deep breath in and let it out with a shudder. It was not healthy to be sitting out here, mulling over all her sorrows. She was getting lost in a miasma of remorse, and she needed to get up now and do something else. As long as she had already lived, Candice was not ready to give up on life yet.

It had been far too long since she had eaten anything substantial, the scone not being nearly enough, so she set about making some food. Once her hunger had been satisfied, her thoughts at last turned to her own concerns that she had set aside in her emotional distress. She still had a problem that had to be dealt with, and since the person she had meant to ask for assistance was now incapacitated, she would either have to figure out a solution herself, or do the unthinkable and approach the only other person she knew who was knowledgeable in the subject. Staring with fear and dread at the chest of drawers that hid the creeping stain within and behind it, Candice bit her lower lip. There was nothing for it. She would have to struggle past her enmity and ask Wilber Tumbleburry for help. She absolutely refused to like doing so, and even determined to give the obnoxious man a piece of her mind before asking him for a favor, deciding he owed her that much given how irritating she had found him over the years.

The walk to Wilber's house was short, but Candice managed to conduct an entire mental argument and compose a long overdue rant in the time it took her to reach his front door. There was so much she wanted to tell the man she had spent so much of her life resenting, so many recriminations and accusations, few with any merit and none of them pleasant. Candice resented his self-importance and his pomposity almost as much as she resented her own jealousy over his friendship with Liola. This man had been a nuisance to her, a drain on Liola's time and attention, a perpetual and incessant intrusion on her friendship, a constant source of pointless questions about the most meaningless of matters. She wanted to curse the man for every inconsequentiality he had inflicted upon Liola's attention and every banal maxim and aphorism he had spouted at every opportunity. Yet, when she looked into his eyes as he opened his door and saw his sadness, a mirror of her own, all her rancor and hatred melted away into a sympathy she never suspected she could feel. His loss was as great as hers, and he had felt it no less than she had. Candice may have never appreciated his friendship with Liola, but it was just as real, just as meaningful, and just as painful. Before she knew what she was doing, Candice had reached out with both arms and ensnared the surprised man in a sympathetic hug. Her request could wait. She would ask him for help, and he would help her like he would have always helped her had she ever asked, but that could wait. They had much to discuss and a mutual friend to commemorate.

After they reluctantly broke apart, both feeling rather awkward and self-conscious once there was air between them, they cast their eyes downward in a mutual moment of silence before Wilber's instincts insisted he invite her inside. They had settled into the plush comfortable chairs in Wilber's living room when the doorbell summoned the home owner once more. Wilber was a hard man to surprise, taking even the more unusual events of his life in stride, but his mind was frazzled and distracted today so the pair of grinning boys holding a box up toward him caught him off guard for a moment. Bobby and the youngest Murphy boy did not seem to mind his hesitation, and just held the box until he took it from their hands. It was addressed to him from Beverly Masterson. Had he been more cognizant and astute at the time, he would have immediately divined the contents of the box, but as he was, Wilber was entirely unsuspecting of the care package he held. Thanking the boys, he went back inside to his guest, setting the mystery package down on a side-table in the entryway to be inspected later.

The boys, having now completed their second mission of the day from Beverly, successfully delivering both this box and the box they had left on Candice's doorstep minutes before, took off at a dead sprint for the schoolteacher's house, fully expecting some manner of reward for their efforts. They were not disappointed in their anticipation, as Beverly had milk and cookies waiting for them. These treats had to wait, however, until they had properly paid obeisance to Lady Nincompoop, who would not allow them inside the Masterson house until she was satisfied. Even the legendary patience of children with animals can be exhausted, and the boys had to resort to a flanking maneuver to get past the demanding cat so they could enter the house and partake of their well earned prize. The whole time they sat at the kitchen table consuming the cookies and milk, the affronted feline whined and mewed at them, snaking around their feet and ankles, occasionally tugging and nipping at their pants legs to demand further pampering. Well acquainted with the inexhaustibility of Lady Nincompoop's desires, Bobby and the youngest Murphy boy had no trouble ignoring her incessant entreaties as they jabbered away about their adventures so far that day. Beverly eventually took pity, on both the cat and the boys, and picked up her needy pet, cuddling the appreciative animal, settling into a chair opposite the boys to enjoy their narrative. The cat purred affectionately even as she occasionally batted at her owners hands, inflicting minor scratches whenever it suited the capricious creature.

As they chatted, somehow the boys' conversation paused when Bobby turned to Beverly and asked, "Say, Ms. Masterson, why're you home today? Don't you have school?"

Many adults would have remonstrated the child for asking impertinent questions of adults, or for being nosy about other people's affairs, but not the veteran schoolteacher. Her philosophy had always been to encourage inquisitiveness in children, especially when the questions were innocuous and innocent. Beverly answered without looking up from her cat, "Not today. I took the day off."

"Huh. I didn't know teachers got days off, 'Cept for summer of course."

"It's 'except' not 'cept', and yes, we get days off every so often. I usually spend mine at my sister's home on the other side of town, but she is traveling right now, so I'm home instead."

"Is that why you were giving out gifts?"

Beverly shook her head, "I would have given the gifts regardless, as the gifts needed to be given. If I had not had the day off, I would have given them out this evening instead."

"Oh. Oh yeah, that makes sense." Like most complicated concepts, the boys only partially grasped social niceties, mostly as far as they had to in order to not face punishment or to stay on friendly terms with all of the various people who occupied their world. The concept that generosity and kindness to those who were not expecting such could be in any way obligatory was beyond their ken, but they nodded and pretended to understand the motivations of one of their favorite adults. After all, there were few adults that understood them as well as Beverly Masterson, and they truly adored her obnoxiously demanding cat.

When the cookies were finished, Beverly insisted they finish the milk in their cups and wash up after themselves before shooing the boys back out into the sunlight to continue their fun and games. They dashed out the door without a backward glance, as assured of her continued existence as they were of everything they ever did. Theirs was a magical age, one without doubts or uncertainties and all the bothersome worries adults always seemed so obsessed with from day to day. Bobby and the youngest Murphy boy were possessed of a self-assurance that can only be borne of those who have never experienced loss, have never seen tragedy, have never had any great disappointments befall them, a self-confidence of those who have not yet grown up. They did not know it, but it was this glowing enthusiasm and surety that endeared them so thoroughly to all that they encountered, and why they could get away with so many trivial devilries so often. As they laughed and played an impromptu game of tag, they ran carelessly down the lane. It was the youngest Murphy boy who suggested they dig up secret 'pirate' treasure.

Bobby shouted his enthusiastic agreement and put on an extra burst of speed, impulsively intent to outrace his best friend to the treasure trove for no specific reason. Darting in-between and around parked cars and rubbish bins as they went, it was a minor miracle that neither child was run down by a passing car or run over by a baby stroller.

They were screeched at by more than one startled mother. It was the youngest Murphy boy who reached the empty strip of land first, but it was both boys together who dug up their small tin box, forgetting in their overexcited state to look about first for anyone who might be observing their activity. Once their concealed treasure trove was exposed and opened, the pair set about verbally indexing the contents. Each boy remarked on every object and where and how they had acquired them in turn. The youngest Murphy boy tried his best to gross out Bobby when he recounted how horridly slimy and squishy the contents of the takeout container had been when he had pulled the collar with the dog tag out of the trash, aggrandizing the awful smell and exaggerating the amount of mold and rot, somehow forgetting Bobby had been present on the occasion in question.

Bobby obligingly acted disgusted, all the while being secretly envious that the youngest Murphy boy had been the one to brave the foul trash to retrieve the dog collar, envious of the bragging rights such an act had earned him. Bobby retrieved and held up the small gold coin with an inquiring and mischievous look in his eyes. The youngest Murphy boy fell silent. This was not a story he wanted to tell, as both boys knew, and the coin, while a prized relic he would never part with for all the world, instilled in him a guilt that was alien. Though he did not know it yet, this guilt would never leave him and would eventually grow into a nagging regret that would haunt him his whole life, as unreasonable and unfounded as it was in his young mind. Suddenly, the youngest Murphy boy was no longer interested in the treasure box or its contents. He began digging idly in the ground next to the hole they hid their box in while Bobby continued to sift through the contents. The youngest Murphy boy nodded idly and replied with short single words whenever his best friend commented about one or another of their prizes. The coin reminded him of the many insignificant iniquities of his life, all of which had been amplified in his consciousness by the irritation and indignation each seemed to cause his parents. His thoughts wandered to all of the unkind comparisons to his older siblings his parents had made, and how inadequate he always seemed to measure in their eyes. His was not a pleasant home life, and it was often that he envied his best friend Bobby and his kind and forgiving family. It was this envy that shamed the youngest Murphy boy whenever he saw the coin, even as he treasured the ill-gotten artifact.

"Hey, what are you kids doing over there?" The question came as a surprise to both of the boys, especially as it was voiced by an adult they did not recognize, and one dressed in some manner of uniform. Their few run-ins with uniformed authority figures so far in their life had instilled an intuitive reticence to trust such people, and an instinctual fear of being discovered doing anything untoward or improper in the presence of such an individual. This particular uniformed individual was advancing on their location with a distinct look of consternation, and both boys panicked. On their feet in an instant, Bobby and the youngest Murphy boy took off at full speed, shouting encouragement at each other as they ran. A full dozen paces down the lane, Bobby realized that neither of them had grabbed their precious treasure box, and turned around to run back, shouting to the youngest Murphy boy as he did, a shout that was not heard by his best friend.

The youngest Murphy boy did not slow down or look back, completely unaware that Bobby had doubled back. He kept running down toward the end of the lane, shouting for Bobby to keep up the whole time. It was only when he spotted Old Mrs. Habernathy, still rooted to the sidewalk in front of her house at the end of the lane and still glowering menacingly in his general direction, that the youngest

Murphy boy skidded to a stop. In the presence of such an aberration in his life, the youngest Murphy boy did not know how to react. He had noticed the old woman standing there at the end of the lane many times over the last few days, as had all of the other residents, but every time he did, it was still jarring and upsetting. There was something off. There was something quite disturbing about the old woman's behavior since she had taken vigil on the side of the street, something far more disquieting and unnerving than at any time before. The air seemed to crackle and shimmer around her, but no one seemed to take notice of the anomaly. Old Mrs. Habernathy herself drew all of their attention and concern. The youngest Murphy boy noticed, and he trembled. In his brief time on this earth, while he had never known serious trouble or travail, he had experienced both fear and pain in some measure. But, as he stared warily at the fierce old lady at the end of the lane, the youngest Murphy boy now knew that what he had experienced so far was not of equal measure to what he could feel rippling out from around her in waves unseen by anyone else.

His eyes wide in growing apprehension, the youngest Murphy boy blinked and looked away, not wanting to see any more of the horrible old woman and her hateful glower. Shaking his head, he opened his eyes once more, but it was not the aged old woman rooted to the sidewalk that filled his gaze now. No, this was something entirely different, something entirely more entrancing than the minacious Old Mrs. Habernathy. His eyes were fixed on the house with the dead yard. All he could see now was the house with the dead yard. All he could feel was the eerie calm of the house with the dead yard. All of his fears and anxieties seemed to dull, then disappear. The youngest Murphy boy was no longer worried about his home life, was no longer concerned about his mother's constant disappointment, was no longer afraid of his father's persistent ire, was no longer burdened by the guilt of his minor larcenies and lies. He was no longer aware of anything but the soft serenity of the house with the dead yard, and the house with the dead yard was summoning him, beckoning him.

He stepped forward, one step then another, each step soothing his mind, each step banishing another thought, another doubt, each step making him surer and surer that the next step should be taken. His eyes unfocused and his vision blurred as the house loomed closer. His ears thudded and thumped as sound other than the coursing of his blood stopped registering. All became silence, even the sudden piercing screeches and curses hurled forth from someone down at the end of the lane. Nothing mattered except the next step, the next step toward the house with the dead yard, and the next step onto the porch of the house with the dead yard, and the next step toward the yawning open door and the darkness beyond, the darkness inside the house with the dead yard, the darkness that was drawing him in, the darkness that would embrace him and comfort him like no other. The youngest Murphy boy could feel at ease now. Soon, soon now, he would not have to feel at all. No tears, no joys, no more anything ever again, good or bad or otherwise. One more step and he would never have to wonder or wander ever after. The youngest Murphy boy stepped forward one more step, across the threshold, past the wide open door, and into the infinite darkness of the house with the dead yard.

Pain, familiar pain, shot through the youngest Murphy boy's shoulder as fingernails dug deeper than should be possible, clawing him back and away from the peace that had been descending upon him. He cried out as he felt himself being yanked and hurled backward, out of the doorway he had been walking through. He was tossed clear through the air to land awkwardly on his back, a few paces from the porch. The youngest Murphy boy blinked and cried from the rough treatment even as he tried to focus his eyes. Through his tears he thought he could see a familiar figure twisting about and struggling with something in the darkness of the doorway, thrashing and fighting with something he could not see at all. Frightened at the spectacle in front of him, the boy was startled even more when the house with the dead yard began vibrating and shuddering, emitting the most awful of sounds, terrible noises that drowned out even the screams and curses of the indistinct individual lashing about in its doorway. Terrified, the youngest Murphy boy did what most small children do in the face of the incomprehensible and the frightening, he closed his eyes and covered his ears against the noises and sights that assaulted him.

The sounds kept coming, each worse than the last, and the youngest Murphy boy began crying out in panic with each new unholy onslaught. He curled up in a ball and called for his mother, whimpering in abject fright. And then there was silence. There were no noises, beyond the usual birds and bugs, and the sound of the wind, and the occasional car from further down the lane. The youngest Murphy boy opened his eyes and looked around. He was alone. He was alone, and he was laying on the ground with his hands over his ears. He was alone, on the ground, and he had no idea why he was there.

"Are you alright, little boy?"

The youngest Murphy boy glanced up and back at the well-dressed middle-aged woman he had never seen before. She was standing on the sidewalk, looking down at him with the same customary concern all adults showed toward him whenever he was distressed or injured. The youngest Murphy boy took his hands away from his ears and, with deliberate care, examined himself all over, trying to honestly assess an answer for the adult. He felt fine. He also felt confused. He had no idea why he was laying on the ground.

Rolling over into a sitting position, then pushing himself up onto his feet, the youngest Murphy boy nodded to the inquisitive adult before darting away down the lane to find Bobby.

Wendy watched the young boy run off with fleeting curiosity. In all of her years in the real estate business, she had seen far more perplexing and puzzling sights than a small child curled up on the ground for no reason. Sighing and resigning herself to never knowing the story behind the little boy's antics, Wendy glanced at her phone to note the time. Her clients were late, which was typical. While she had never dealt with these particular clients before, she had spent many hours of her adult life waiting on others who had far looser definitions of punctuality than herself, all of which she had learned to bear without complaint. It did not pay in her trade to express dissatisfaction with those she was trying to earn a commission from. As she waited, Wendy checked over the salient details of the lot in front of her for the dozenth time, committing the few items of interest to memory so that she would not need to refer to the printed information when pitching the property to her clients.

She looked up at the sound of someone running and stepped back off the sidewalk to allow the young woman to jog past her, reflexively raising her hand to return the offered high-five as she passed. This out of the ordinary greeting gave the seasoned professional pause, and a wry, bemused grin spontaneously broke her world-weary expression. Wendy did not have long to contemplate the incident however, as a car pulled up and parked next to her. Putting on her well-practiced smile, Wendy greeted George and Amanda as they got out of the car, even offering a helping hand to the very pregnant young woman.

After the sociable pleasantries were properly exchanged, George furrowed his brow as he studied the lot they were standing in front of for the first time, commenting, "Are we sure this is the right place?"

"Yes, definitely the correct address. Why?"

"Well, I mean. I've never seen a vacant lot so well landscaped. I thought you said there was no owner?"

"Absolutely. This is being sold by the municipality. No prior owner was found, so they annexed it and now it is available for private ownership."

"So who is mowing the lawn and pruning the trees?"

Wendy looked at the well-manicured lawn and the recently cut branches of the trees on the empty lot she was trying to sell. It did look far too cared for. Turning back to her clients, she answered what she normally did when she was unsure of something, "I will look into that."

Amanda touched her father's arm gently and pointed broadly at all of the other houses on the lane around them, remarking, "I bet it is one of the neighbors. I mean, have you ever seen so many lovely gardens?"

George nodded as he eyed the topiaries and flowerbeds of the surrounding yards, "Yeah, I bet that's it. They seem to be pretty serious about it here."

Amanda smiled appreciatively, "I like it! So beautiful!"

Wendy kept smiling, her clients seemed to be selling themselves, which she would be a fool to interrupt. Once the father and daughter had satisfied themselves as to the nature of their potential neighbors, Wendy conducted them around the empty lot, pointing out the utility hookups and indicating the property lines and the specifics of the setbacks they would have to keep in mind if they purchased the place and built a house there. There was the usual round of questions and answers about the available amenities in the area, and Wendy was astute enough to note the nearby park and the easy access to public transportation services. They were interrupted by the immediate next door neighbor introducing himself to the prospective new homeowners, a pleasant surprise that Wendy could have kissed the amenable old academic for. The professorly scholar did much to recommend the lane to her clients, and she stood a short pace aback so as to put no pressure on either party to end the conversation. Inevitability, the neighbor of the empty lot was called away by another neighbor from further down the lane, and he hurried off at an ungainly pace, leaving Wendy and her clients alone once more. After a few more particulars were addressed, they agreed to meet at her office the following day to prepare an offer on the lot, and to discuss the permits they would need to apply for to start construction once the sale went through.

Wendy waved goodbye as George and Amanda climbed back into their car and started to drive away, only to shout in warning for them to stop as a small puppy ran directly out into the road in front of them. Their vehicle braked in time and the puppy ran on, oblivious to the danger it had put itself in, barking in excitement at the little girl and the two young boys, one of which was the child from earlier, chasing it down the lane. The trio of children and the small pet vanished around one of the houses near the end of the lane before George started driving away again, giving another wave goodbye to their now nervous real estate agent. Wendy breathed a sigh of relief as she watched their car turn down one of the adjoining roads off the lane. Checking the time on her phone once more, she noted she still had another thirty minutes before she needed to leave for her next appointment elsewhere. Breathing in deeply, she relaxed a bit. This really was a pleasant neighborhood, and the abundant varieties of flowering plants created a cacophony of agreeable odors.

In a rare instance of extemporization in her tightly regimented life, Wendy decided to go for a quick walk around the lane. As she was already near the end of the cul-de-sac, she chose to go the long way around, examining each of the charming gardens along the way, marveling at the creativity and individuality of each of the yards. The one festooned with pink pelican statues stood out as an unfathomably unfashionable exception to the otherwise uniform excellence. Wendy found herself being charmed by the lane and all of its residents, several of whom introduced themselves to her unbidden, a few even offering her freshly baked muffins or pastries. She made a note to inquire as to the owner of one house she was informed had left to travel the world, to see if he would be interested in renting his house through her while he was away. The further she walked around the lane, the more entranced by the neighborhood she became. If she were not already twenty years into a thirty year mortgage on her own home across town, Wendy would have given serious thought to putting in an offer on her own behalf for the vacant lot.

Having walked to the far end of the lane, where it intersected and vanished into the other streets of the suburb, and walked all the way back along the other side of the street, Wendy was approaching the end of the cul-de-sac when she first saw it. There, at the very end of the lane, sat a lot with a seemingly vacant house, overgrown with weeds and feral landscaping. There were no signs it had ever been lived in, and in amongst its well groomed neighbors, appeared entirely out of place. Wendy stopped walking as she took in the sight, studying the structure, ascertaining that it was sound and habitable at least from its outward appearance.

Hearing voices to the side of her, Wendy turned to observe the scholarly neighbor from before struggling to carry a large and unwieldy object with an older woman out of the home next to the abandoned house. It was an unwieldy chest of drawers which appeared to be covered in some strange orange powder and ash. Waiting for them to reach the curb and deposit their burden next to the rubbish bins, Wendy waved to them and asked, "Do you know who owns that place?"

The pair looked at where she pointed, but they both shrugged, looking confused, almost as if they had never seen the place before, as impossible as that would have been. She tried a different question, "Has anyone lived there recently?"

The academic she had met prior was the one to answer, though the woman he was with nodded agreement at his words, "I don't recall that anyone has ever lived there."

The preposterousness of this statement seemed obvious only to Wendy, but she thanked the pair and turned back to the house without voicing protest. It would be ludicrous for a house on a lane so well appointed and affluent to remain vacant for so long. It was just unheard of. Surely there had to be an explanation. Perhaps a search of the local municipality records for occupancy or ownership would satisfy her curiosity. She was about to turn away, to head back to her car and leave the lane, when she noticed another oddity. The front door of the vacant house with the feral landscaping was ajar. Wendy approached the vacant house, peering at the windows, trying to discern anything within through the dirty panes, to no avail. Yes, the door was ajar, standing open a foot or so, but even as she got closer, she could not see anything within through the gap.

Wendy did not know why the urge struck her, but she suddenly wanted to enter the house, to look around, perhaps to evaluate its salability, or perhaps just to snoop. She should have known better, she did know better. Even if it were not a matter of trespass to enter the vacant house, her common sense would have told her it was possible there were vagrants or squatters inside, and that it was dangerous to go inside. She was not reckless, her life was a series of cautious and calculated events and decisions with as few risks as possible, one she had done her best to live with a healthy regard to her own well being and safety. She stood on the porch, twisting her head around, trying to contort the laws of physics to allow her to see around the solid door, to see beyond the blank wall visible in the gap between the jamb and the door that stood free of its latch. She would just take a quick look, she told herself. Somewhere inside the vacant house, several clocks chimed to herald the evening hour.

The last rays of the sun to touch the lane that day disappeared beneath the trees and rooftops as Wendy slowly pushed the door open and stepped inside.

Author's Note

I hope you have enjoyed reading Once Upon a Lane. It was a pleasure to write and I hope as much of a pleasure to read. If you would like others to know what you think of the story, I would appreciate if you left a review on any of the venues online that allow for that, and if you inform others of this book by means of your favorite medium of communication, be it social, personal, or otherwise. Your help in spreading the word of what you enjoy reading is always appreciated by any author, and especially by me. I look forward to bringing you more stories in the future, and thank you for reading.

You can find more of my stories at my homepage: https://hicsuntdeos.com/

Made in the USA
Columbia, SC
31 October 2024

45412055R00100